LATER WHEN THE TIDE COMES IN

DAVID LASSWELL

Author's Tranquility Press
MARIETTA, GEORGIA

David Lasswell/Author's Tranquility Press
2706 Station Club Drive SW
Marietta, GA 30060
www.authorstranquilitypress.com

Publisher's Note: This is a work of fiction. Names, characters, places, and incidents are a product of the author's imagination. Locales and public names are sometimes used for atmospheric purposes. Any resemblance to actual people, living or dead, or to businesses, companies, events, institutions, or locales is completely coincidental.

Ordering Information:
Quantity sales. Special discounts are available on quantity purchases by corporations, associations, and others. For details, contact the "Special Sales Department" at the address above.

LATER WHEN THE TIDE COMES IN/David Lasswell
Paperback: 978-1-958554-88-3
eBook: 978-1-958554-89-0

FOREWORD

You are holding a book of fiction written by a recognized author, a wordsmith, and a believable storyteller. LATER WHEN THE TIDE COMES IN is a fictitious story of poverty, government failures, and uncertain futures. It is also a story of lasting friendships, truths, partnering, love and life's pleasures and enjoyments.

LATER WHEN THE TIDE COMES IN, was written to increase the awareness of poverty on the World-Stage with hopes someone, somewhere, sometime soon, would do something about it.

It is a major travesty that governments haven't invested an effort to get rid of poverty. This is not only an American problem but is an issue in over eighty-seven percent of the countries known to man.

The fictitious company Providers, imagined in Saint Petersburg in Florida, brings awareness to poverty in and on nearly every continent. The primary characters throughout the book have been factiously created. But the persona and personalities of my real-life family and friends are blended throughout.

Locations, schools, colleges and universities are real and do exist. In addition, throughout the book, non-fiction facts and people will play a short part and will appear in the writing.

I wanted to publicly acknowledge this fact: The majority of the story is made up by the author and a few of his silly but loving, faithful friends.

DEDICATION

To the citizens of the world, regardless of nationalities, homeland, location and condition, who are lacking support, care and security; this book is dedicated to you.

Poverty must end. We must all love and remember the have nots. Many individuals who have lost the desire, hope, and spirit, have experienced unexpected circumstances.

The author wishes you well and to succeed and offers a prayer for you to overcome your current standing in life. May you all be blessed. DL.

Contents

PROLOGUE: *IDAHO'S FINEST*

Have you ever been to Boise? Yes, the one in Idaho. Now famous for potatoes. People say it is easy to get to Boise from any direction on Interstate 84, from the West or the East. Maybe that's the North or the South? Regardless where you start from, it's worth the trip.

I didn't get to Boise by car. I was carried in Boise by my pregnant mother for nine months. In a court document, for the purpose of giving me up for adoption, she wrote and signed a statement which said she was not attacked, raped, or taken by an unwanted lover. What do you expect from someone who enjoyed the experience?

However, this is what you don't expect from a well-built, blue-eyed blond, nineteen-year-old, somewhat known as being on the wild-side? Who didn't understand the word: protection?

When she found out she was pregnant, after cussing and screaming for some time, reported she didn't want anything to do with motherhood.

My father had given my mother an erroneous name before the one-night-stand that lasted a day and one-half. My father, after one phone call to my mother later, was told she was pregnant. He got out of Dodge as fast as he could, probably on I-84; your choice of direction.

End result, I would be put up for adoption at the time of my birth. That's where my life's story begins.

CHAPTER ONE:
THE BEGINNING

My birth mother's name was Lilly Anne Lavender. She was a young woman, somewhat strange. A woman whose' drummer beat differently than most. Thankfully, she didn't believe in abortions. She stood in my corner for nine-month. At the time of birth, she stopped our relationship.

I was adopted by my birth mother's older sister and her husband; Avery and Florence Fox. At the time of adoption both my new mother and father were in their late twenties.

My adoptive parents had the court approve them naming me—the baby. It is true that I was not given a name at birth but nearly two weeks later.

My birth certificate listed my father as black: name—unknown. I am identified on my birth certificate as Caucasian. I was born on November 23, 1970. I was delivered, so to speak, at Saint Alphonsus Hospital, in beautiful Boise.

Since my birth, there is now 'one' in Boise soon to be more famous than the potato. I could have been called Spud. Sorry, for the humor. Dad and mom Fox had been in Boise for three days completing the adoption papers after seven months of labor getting it done. Please accept the pun.

My new parents didn't reside in Boise, but in the sailor's town of Bremerton on Puget Sound, in the Evergreen State of Washington. Just a fifty-minute ferry ride from Seattle.

The distance between Boise and Bremerton is just over five hundred and fifty miles. Normally, about nine hours of driving time but not when you have an infant in the car needing diapers changed and Similac formula heated before being ready for a hungry infant.

I had plenty of sleep heading further into the Northwest. I had a comfortable infant's bed in the backseat of my mother's 1968 Chevy Civic. My father was the designated driver, my mother was the designated caregiver and I was the designated center of attention everywhere we stopped.

I was just a week old and already spoiled. That didn't last long. My adopting dad was a teacher at Olympic Junior College and up until the adoption my mother was a secretary working in the Bremerton Naval Ship Yard.

I was given the distinguished name of Silas Franklyn Fox. I have no clue as to whom I was named after. I will add the word Sir at a later date.

Later, I was told that Silas means; the man of the forest—or fuel of the fire.

When I was eight years old, my mother told me that her sister and my birth mother died of a drug overdose in San Francisco about eight months after I was born. How sad.

We lived in Bremerton on the Sound until I was in the eighth grade going to Dewey Junior High. I was good at running between the raindrops. Barely a drop on my crew-cut hair style.

When I was in junior high, my mother spent a lot of time selling-the-point: don't cut corners. Don't take the easy way out. Do what you are asked to do and do more than what you said you would do.

That goes for making your bed and cleaning your room, watering the garden, mowing the lawn, raking the leaves, doing your homework, preparing for a test and being gracious and kind to any female: girl, young woman or lady you will meet sometime throughout your life.

My mother added. Teachers and others must be able to say, "Silas is well mannered." I always wondered if she coached my dad too. My mother was genuine.

My father applied and was accepted for a position in Moscow at the University of Idaho. He became a Professor of International Policies and Foreign Affairs. He was now Doctor Fox after earning his PhD at the dawg-pound at the U of Washington.

During my high school years, I went to Moscow High School, the home of the Bears. I centered my concentration on studies, debate, speech contests and other school competitions. As a non-jock, I was accepted on the popular side of the student body. I was built like one, but I didn't play like one. I had no game.

Between my junior and senior years, I was selected to go to Boys State. How? That's hard to say. Many other Juniors, including friends, were more qualified. I did not care. While there for a week on the campus of Idaho State University, I first truly learned about the American political system. I learned enough that I wasn't interested in a political future.

I had many friends among the jocks, bookworms and nerds. I liked them all and they liked and supported me with my studies. My two very favorite non-dating female friends; Sharon and Nancy would listen and provide me with pointers on prepared remarks needed for my debates and speech contests.

Both girls were extremely nice and brilliant. Sharon was from Port Orchard and Nancy from

Port Angeles in Washington State. Both dads worked at the university.

After fighting a long, tough battle with ovarian cancer, my mother died three weeks before my high school graduation. She was still pretty at forty-four-years-of-age.

My mother was a professional in the kitchen. She was an exceptional cook and baker and my dad and I marveled at her loyalty of preparation of the master-menu's she created.

There was never a day that went by that she didn't have a smile on her face. Her glass was always half full, never half empty. If it was raining, mother would say tomorrow will be a better day. Rain always falls before the rainbow appears.

I remember the very last thing she told me. Remember Silas, you always have to prepare for what comes next.

The second worst feeling I had in my life was when my adopted sister from Taiwan was kidnapped from our elementary school in Bremerton in broad daylight. The story made national news when I was ten-years-old.

It was a typical day, the two of us were dropped off by our father at the Crownhill Elementary School like any other day. I saw my little-sister walk into the school with her friends before me. I haven't seen her since. Her bedroom at the house was like a 'do not-pass zone.' It was untouched for probably a year.

The story basically is this. An oriental man who carried forged documents went to the school office to pick up my sister about nine o'clock in the morning. The staff said my sister must have known the man for she ran and jumped into his arms. Everything looked normal to them. Believing their story is not easy. But I try.

The family didn't know about this until it was time to pick us up at two-forty in the afternoon. We all were heartbroken. My mother cried for days as did I.

The FBI was called in immediately. It is considered a cold case now. It is closed in our minds. Nothing came of the long search that followed. My parents thought about going to Taiwan but decided against it. Something about sand going down a knot hole.

The school wanted me to change to another elementary school location in Kitsap County. Orchard Heights grade school in Port Orchard knew of the incident and accepted me in. I was there through the sixth grade. I had great teachers.

My mother was a smaller woman, not fragile; not over five-feet-four-inches tall and was a devout Christian who also loved to paint, do quilts, sew and designed the interior of our house beautifully. She is still being missed. Her design remains.

I went through with all of the ceremonies with my graduation. I knew my mother would have wanted that. My father told me how much he loved me and the two of us would get through this hard time and do well in the future.

My father was shorter than six feet, maybe five-feet-eleven. His weight was in the neighborhood of one-sixty-eight. He had a lovely tenor voice, who many times sang solos in our church.

When he spoke, he was very easy to listen to and was talented in his delivery style. He sounded like Paul Harvey from the radio. And that's my story, his story follows. We were both very proud of what we achieved.

CHAPTER TWO:
GETTING TO KNOW DAD

My dad loved music from almost any era from the 'swing' of the forties to the 'rock-n-roll' of the late fifties and sixties. Often, he listened to big band numbers on the vinyl and then switched to military medleys and marches.

I can remember going into his study and he would sit in his recliner thinking he was the conductor of the sound being played. I think my dad knew every lyric from the musical sound of the late fifties.

He thought the 'Platters' were the absolute best. He liked all artists; he didn't care, man or woman, groups, black or white. Sam Cook was one of his favorites too. He later learned to love country music.

I graduated number sixteen in a class of two-hundred-and-seventy-eight. The girls controlled eleven of the first fifteen positions. I was satisfied with my placement and I knew my national test scores would allow me to go just about any place I could afford to go to college. Study didn't make Silas a 'dull' boy.

I thought I wanted to go to a small college and I looked into many. Alaska Pacific University in Anchorage; Whitworth University in Spokane, John Fox University in Portland and even some schools in California. Out-of-state costs were out of sight.

Instead, I listened to my father's advice and stayed home and went to the University of Idaho, and I became a proud Vandel. I majored in journalism and mass communications. My minor was in public and international affairs. I once thought about switching majors, but I didn't want to lose credits.

I had an advantage over other students in International Studies for my father allowed me to read his notes prepared for him teaching international foreign affairs and I stayed up-to-date on issues of countries in the world. Yes, it helped.

I learned one major fact in college. If the people of the world were allowed to visit, mix and mingle, the world would be better off. But there will always be a North Korea, Cuba, Iran or others getting in the way and stopping progress.

I graduated with honors from the University of Idaho in June 1994. I didn't make the President's distinguished list of scholars but the Dean's 'Quality' List. Honestly, I achieved this with the help of two delightful, lovely young women.

One was a beautiful international exchange student from Sweden. Her name was Olga Olsen. The other was an equally beautiful black woman from Detroit. Her name was Savannah Jade. I truly was attracted to and appreciated both of them, but they were very close friends and when you saw one; you saw the other.

I did not have the heart to step in between them. If I had, I would have seriously dated Savannah and probably in time, would have wanted to ask her to be my wife. She was far different than others and I am not talking about her being black.

I would have been scolded, laughed at and ridiculed for thinking such thoughts. I can hear the questions now: how well do you know her? What do you know about her? And how and why would a mixed racial situation sit with your family and friends? At our ages, I thought I knew both of us well. I was an idiot.

Jake, one of my jock friends: wasn't kind in saying what he said. "Savannah is very lovely; but there is far more to a woman than her smile and body." Perhaps, I was influenced by those. Forget the 'perhaps.

Savannah's companion Olga, had many admirers but seldom ever dated. Many lookers who didn't have the time or the money. You can imagine a lovely blond from Stockholm, Sweden.

I know I was appreciated by both, but I guess it is true I was their adopted security-blanket at a university with many handsome men and glorious ladies.

You didn't see color first when you looked at Savannah. She had sparkle within even within a somewhat darken room. Sweet, kind, considerate, polite and smart as a whip.

Her dad was a motor-city police officer. A high-ranking police sergeant who had been on the force for years. Her mother is an ICU nurse working in Garden City, just outside of Detroit. Her mother too was small in stature but bigger-than-life in care, love and talents in taking care of others. Savannah looked a lot like her mother.

If my mother would have lived, she would have liked and appreciated Savannah but would have been against me considering marriage. The location of her upbringing in Klamath Falls, Oregon, I guess would have made her think that.

My dad on the other hand, who maintains a balanced life, believes in character and their common sense, attitude and the inter-driving spirit making up an individual's life.

Both Olga and Savannah majored in elementary education. Both loved children with desires to work with kids to get them off the street, into the classrooms, and further into books of learning. They both graduated with me.

After graduation, Olga went back to Sweden and taught school in Stockholm caring for less-gifted elementary students. Savannah, had more than one offer and chose to teach in Livonia. At Idaho, I was not a lesson of elementary life.

After the U of I, I found an excellent salaried job. I worked there for one year. You would recognize the name of the National-Fortune-Five-Hundred Company. I should have looked further for a position and a company that would have appreciated my efforts.

My dad certainly knew about the trend for liberals in our schools, universities and corporate giants. As an individual, my father was a conservative. Let's say center or moderate. He thought like Ronald Reagan.

My thoughts were told to my dad and he told me there was only one thing to do. Join the branch of service you want and enjoy the military for one enlistment. The military, dad spoke, "will do you some good." Within a week, I had seen four of the branches' recruiters: Army, Navy, Air Force and Marines. I loved the water, but no Coast Guard.

I studied the opportunities of going enlisted or entering to become an officer. I chose the United States Marines Corps. I would become an enlisted jarhead. It was a month's wait before heading to basic training at Parris Island, South Carolina. I made a great choice. It was tough becoming a member of the Few, the Proud, the Marines.

The Marines made me a man as my dad said it would. I loved the Corps. I reached the rank of E-four when I was discharged in the early Spring of 2001 after proudly serving this great country for six years. I stood for our Flag and Anthem. I still do and I always will.

It is hard to believe but a single person in the military can save money. When I left the Marines, I had more than a small-nest-egg where I could spend some time thinking and preparing before my next assignment in life.

I talked to my dad and told him I wanted to lay back for a couple of months and see what developed as I relaxed. He told me, "Go for it." He also said, "I bet you are going to Seabeck."

CHAPTER THREE:
THE BEST KEPT SECRET

I went back to the waters of Puget Sound to a small, quaint-little community of Seabeck. The water and boats were beautiful and the fishing was graded triple-A. I was hooked there. Along with the salmon.

Seabeck had charm that a larger community doesn't have. I went to a little Chapel in Lonerock, not far back down the road. Seabeck had a beautiful primrose garden called Collin's Gardens. It's on the road toward Holly.

There is also a Conference Grounds for summer religious education. I walked across the bridge and toured the facilities. One of the best walks I ever took in my life. I walked past people with smiling faces and warm greetings. The gestures were welcomed.

There is so much more to Seabeck: the people, the kindness and the togetherness that's hard to find in America. They share with neighbors who know that someday they will have to be able to use something. Don't be surprised if you are ever in Seabeck that a complete stranger doesn't volunteer to buy your lunch.

One day on the bulletin board at the General Store, I read a note that said I have to make two short stops in Silverdale; my name is Jeff. Do you have room for me in your car and for the trip back?

It was in Seabeck when I received a request for money from PROVIDERS OF INTERNATIONAL CARE AND EDUCATION. When I opened the envelope, I knew it was not going to be junk mail.

I read the enclosed letter and brochure and decided to write the check. On their enclosed paper, I wrote I am mailing this check because I believe in your company's mission.

It is hard to believe what happened. About three weeks later, I received a letter from Mister Blake Tate, the Human Resource Director from PROVIDERS, and the letter said if I had international interests, I would be invited to a ten-day seminar in St. Petersburg, Florida all expenses paid. That opened my eyes.

The letter pointed out there would be eight people receiving similar letters. The letter added that the company could hire perhaps as many as four. I was convinced I should attend. The dates would be September Eight through the Seventeenth of September 2001.

I was intrigued. Who were the other seven, what were their backgrounds and where were they from? I was excited. But I have to admit, I went back to my fishing. I rowed my boat off from shore. The fish must have been in school all day without recess, and I was skunked.

It was hard to concentrate on anything but the departure date. A lot was done in preparation of going. Clothes, personal care items, and the study of human awareness of others. I read this book on Human Awareness with the idea of wanting to know more about how a company like Providers would select candidates.

The book also gave me an insight of personalities and profiles of others and how to judge character and not to decide if I liked the people or not because of what they looked like and how they acted towards me.

I was living a dream and who knows what will develop. Even my dad was interested in my welfare and asked many questions in my preparation.

The FedEx package arrived two days ago with information and all of my tickets. The company had spent a great sum of money and I looked forward to dazzle them.

I was riding on a cloud during the bus ride from Seabeck to Bremerton. The ferry from Bremerton to Seattle and finally the taxi ride again to the Seattle-Tacoma Airport. It was Friday afternoon and I stayed at a hotel at the airport.

It was really a crazy scene at the hotel on that Friday evening. People checking out after five, people checking in. In the dining room, some people were eating steaks and others enjoying scrambled eggs and toast. You could tell which ones had a long night ahead of them.

I was up before the sun. Yes, there is sun in Seattle. I was at the airport check-in just minutes before six o'clock. Part of the trip was flying with Alaska Airlines to Denver. Then United Airlines to Florida. The women who sat by the window had to go potty probably six times between Denver and the South. I traded seats with her, I had the window; she had the aisle.

Provider's, the company had sent a car for me in Tampa and the drive down to St. Petersburg was splendid.

CHAPTER FOUR:
FINE IN FLORIDA

My check-in at the Fairfield Inn and Suites was smooth and the accommodations were beyond nice. I am here, ready, prepared and very excited. This has been one 'hell' of a Saturday. It is now six o'clock in the evening and the welcome social is only two hours away.

When my room was organized, I went to the lobby and found a comfortable easy chair facing the check-in counters. I was studying the people. Then I realized there was a lovely woman standing before me. She said I had taken her chair.

When I started to get up, she stopped me and said she was only kidding. She took the easy chair beside me and asked, "if I was doing the same as she?" My answer was maybe.

She introduced herself as Asia Lynn Dash. "I was invited by Providers." "How about you?" Ditto, I told her. She added. "I could tell that you were one of the eight."

Asia was a knock-out. She has the most beautiful blond hair, cut and curled to her shoulders. Her pretty face was highlighted by her dancing blue eyes. She said she was of British and Welch descent. I didn't care; she was also a fox.

"Where are you from?" she asked. My home is in "God's Country" in Washington State. She mentioned she was from Grand Junction, Colorado and had just a couple of months earlier had retired from the United States Air Force.

I thanked her for her service to our country and said I am a former Marine. Both of us would learn more information at tomorrow morning opening session.

We continued to talk for a few minutes when we were interrupted by a well-manicured, dark brown person who introduced himself as Horatio Geronimo Nightcloud.

He mentioned he was a twenty-five percent Osage Native American from the four-corner area of Colorado. He was another one of the eight.

The next person who stopped by to chat was about five-foot-eight, looked very athletic, said she was from Valdez, Alaska and was now an FBI agent out of the Seattle office. Her name was Katarina Grace Damaris. Ms. Asia Lynn said, "She is a live wire with her flaming red hair and green eyes." Another of the eight.

I couldn't believe my eyes. Walking toward us was a woman I knew and deeply believed in while at the University of Idaho. Savannah Jade, I greeter her with a smile. Savannah said she was now living and working in Livonia, Michigan. When she saw me the first thing that I heard her say was, "as I live and breathe".

Now, I know of five of the eight. Three more to meet and greet.

Soon another black woman walked in our direction. Her dark eyes were sparkling and her gait was well-rehearsed and she looked as professional as they come. "Hello," she said. "My name is Della Faye Sharp. Who are you and your pretty friend?" I answered the best I could just after seeing Savannah.

Next to meet was a former All-American black football player from the University of Texas, Alan Arnold Carpenter. A former Longhorn football tailback who severely injured both knees and ended his college athletic career in his junior year. We will have to have some time to have some private conversations this week. He agreed.

The last to meet was a character. He was about six-feet two, two-hundred and ten pounds and a smile that would melt anyone he talked with. He was all muscle from the University of Wyoming was Jasper Levi Crawford. He wanted to stand out and he did. Wearing a plaid shirt, blue jeans and cowboy boots.

I believe his belt buckle costs several hundred dollars. Jasper spoke with such quality and vocabulary you might have thought he came from Georgetown or Harvard. I can't wait for his speech tomorrow.

Savannah Jade and I, after the reception, walked back to the lobby, sat there and talked for about one hour.

CHAPTER FIVE:
IT'S STARTED

Opposite the eight candidates' tables arranged in a half-moon shape were two tables together facing the visitors. On each end of the company's table were hired women court recorders and their equipment. Seated next to Mr. Blake Emerson Tate was a lovely Latino photographer named Louise.

"Please come in and find your table," Mr. Tate said.

To be seated at table one was Katarina Grace Damaris, working in Seattle. At table two was Horatio Geronimo Nightcloud, from Colorado now working in Albuquerque. At table three was Asia Lynn Dash, recently retired from the United States Air Force. I sat in Table four, with my eyes on table three.

Seated at table five was Savannah Jade Whitlock, from Michigan. At table six was Alan Arnold Carpenter, raised in Texas and living in San Antonio. Seated at table seven was Della Faye Sharp, from Greenville, and living in Charleston. Finally, was Jasper Levi Crawford, from Chugwater, Wyoming working a ranch life near Cheyenne.

"Before we officially begin, I will ask Louise to take a smiling and a non-smiling picture of each of you." Louise, a beautiful Latino woman, was through with the project in just a flash. No pun intended. Without saying a word, Mr. Tate walk in front of our tables looking at each of us intently. He acted like a bulldog. He returned to his chair. Louise was excused.

For about the next ten minutes we listened to Mr. Tate. Basically, this is what he said. I have some statistical facts I need to pass along.

When I walked in front of your tables and took a long hard look at you; no one blinked. That is always a professional sign of internal strength. So far, his bark was worse than his bite.

All eight of you listed on your report form you were an extrovert. All eight of you have written that you are Christian. Only one of you is now married. Two others have previously been married; one is divorced and one is a widow. Asia, I am sorry for the loss of your husband. God bless the men who fly and fight.

Your total average grade point in high school was a three-point-seven-six, and from university, records averaged together was a three-point-five-four GPA.

We have six Republicans in the group and two Independents. You live and work in the West, Midwest and South. None of you are from the

East. Several of you have traveled overseas and only Asia and Horatio have worked overseas while in the Air Force and Navy. You other former military members mentioned favorite overseas locations but not living there.

We are a company of diversity. You represent the great Country of America. All eight of you are proud Americans. We have three black candidates and one white male with a black father, name unknown. We have three additional white and a twenty-five-percent Osage Native American.

Something I am most proud of in this group is most of you graduated from relatively small colleges: Alaska Anchorage, two of you from Idaho, one from Pacific University, Wyoming, Maryland, Furman, Texas and Gonzaga. Again, no one from the East. For some reason, folks in Eastern states don't donate like others.

"Let me talk about your speeches. Don't spend time giving us praise. I have had previous candidates talk as little as five minutes, most about ten minutes. I won't let you go longer than that." "I will learn your life story later."

"Other thoughts, you were all above ninety-percentile in scoring in our tests. One of you scored 98-percent and another 96-percent and others between 90 and 95-percent." "We believe you honestly took the tests without assisted help and returned the test package to my office by

overnight mail. The test was not a 'piece of cake'."
"It wasn't designed to be easy." "It told us what we
needed to know."

"This is how the speeches will be given:
number one, eight, two, seven, three, six, four, and
five. Yes, you guessed right. You are speaking in
order with the highest score first." I had the
seventh highest score. I am not a test taker.

"Finally, there is not one of you who is not
worthy of being here. You all should be proud.
After the final speech presentation today, we will
talk briefly about the rest of the course and the
hiring process."

Our offices are here in Saint Petersburg
because of the weather. Now we have people in
eight countries. Working on behalf of local
residents. Those numbers will increase in the near
future.

"We will take a fifteen-minute recess and
come back and get started." We were all in our
assigned seats on time. All but Mr. Tate.
Eventually, he showed.

Mr. Tate invited us to take notes. "Ms.
Damaris, you are first. Please remain seated but do
use the microphone in front of you."

Katarina Grace Damaris began with opening
remarks. "Honestly, I am not totally surprised

about my ninety-eight score. I was a Mensa in college."

"I was born in Valdez, Alaska in the fall of 1970 to Demetrius and Donna Damaris. My parents owned a small tourist business and in my teenage years I became a white-water rafting guide. I fear nothing, no one, and I proudly serve my country."

"I graduated from Valdez High School in 1988. We were the Buccaneers and our school colors were black and blue. The teams we played were like that too. I grew in height to five-foot-seven and I am very athletic, strong and capable of defending myself following difficult training."

"I have from the University of Alaska Anchorage a degree in criminal justice in 1992. I also have a law degree from Gonzaga in Spokane in early 1996. I was accepted and completed the twenty-week course with the FBI at the Marine Training Base in Quantico, Virginia."

"One of my instructors called me a hard ass with an attitude. In some way, he didn't know what he was talking about. In other ways, he did. I know some martial arts and I have a qualified expert with many military-style weapons. I am a sniper."

"I live on Bainbridge Island and commute to Seattle by ferry every morning and evening. I return home also by ferry." "I am a full-fledged FBI agent out of Seattle." "If you haven't noticed,

I have natural red hair with green eyes; I am single. I am a very strong Christian who communicates with my God on a daily basis. God is very big in my life for several reasons, one being the dangers in my job."

"I would love to combine your position with my FBI career and protect our crew from dangers anywhere in the world. Thank you."

"Next up is Jasper Levi Crawford."

"Good morning. I am honored to be before you. I want you all to know about the clothes I wear in Wyoming and why they make great sense. You don't have to wear a three-piece suit to be successful." "You might call me a dude; other mid-westerners call me typical Wyoming." "I am proud of that."

"In Wyoming, we call our shoes boots; not cowboy boots. Most of our boots cover about four to ten inches above our ankles and protect us from critters on the ground." "There are many." "Some will scare the 'hell' out of you."

"Our leather chaps or leggings protect us from snake strikes and the bad and dangerous poison weeds on the ranch. Our plaid shirts with the long sleeves are designed to go under and up into the gloves I wear gloves on both hands."

"For the hat, it serves many purposes. The front bill of the hat help keeps the sun and or the rain out of our eyes and face. The rear and sides of the hat protect against the bright sun and bad weather. The long gaucho-coats help keep us dry and warm."

"I say this because Wyoming is out-west but not out of touch with the country or the world." "You all could be educated if you came and visited Wyoming."

"My education at the University of Wyoming compares to any of yours or your achievements. I scored ninety-six on our test and I am proud of it. I spent eight years in the United States Army and left the service only to take care of the ranch when my father died. I, too am single."

"I love country music and I enjoy line-dancing. We have a ranch foreman and six cowpokes who work hard and diligently. The ranch is called the Diamond-Stud Ranch and is located thirty-eight miles northwest of Cheyenne."

"I would be proud to be offered a position with Providers and would give great thought and considering of accepting. Thank you."

"Horatio Geronimo Nightcloud."

"I was born in Lewis, Colorado in the far-southern corner of Colorado. My parents are Rubin and Guadalupe Nightcloud. I was educated in the small city of Cortez, Colorado, where I played four high school sports."

"I actually excelled in mathematics. I earned a college math scholarship to the University of Pacific in their department of physics. After college, I applied and received a direct commission in the United States Navy. I was assigned to the Naval Submarine Base, Bangor, Washington."

"I spent six very happy and productive years spending much time overseas in European countries of Spain, Greece, and Italy, to name just a few. I met my wife Priscilla while in Spain and we were married in Barcelona. We have two boys and two girls."

"I am currently employed by the US Department of Energy in Albuquerque, New Mexico. I intend to provide service to my country in any way possible. Thank you."

"Ms. Della Faye Sharp."

"I was in the small minority of black students at Furman University in Greenville, South Carolina. But I graduated with honors with a BA Degree in Small Business Administration. My minor was in Corporate Finance."

"My hometown is Greenville; I work in Charleston. I have been connected to Greenville all of my life. My dad was stationed at Donaldson Air Force Base and retired there when Donaldson was closed in 1963."

"Race has never been an issue with me. There are people of different skin colors and religious preferences that I like and others of the same I don't respect, understand, acknowledge or appreciate."

"But those are few in number."

"I financially support organizations worldwide whose missions is to bring people forward with a hand up but not a handout. I would fit in nicely with Providers."

"My mother Alice Jane is still alive and my father is deceased. I have concentrated on my career and not finding a husband. I am still single. Mr. 'Right' hasn't appeared as yet; furthermore, I am not looking."

"Perhaps my greatest achievement was entering and completing a difficult 'charm' school when I learned how to walk, act, speak and socially participate. In a nutshell, that is how I got here today."

"I have been fascinated by your thoughts, ideas and stories. Thank you."

"Ms. Asia Lynn Dash."

"My parents loved everything oriental, thus my name."

"I lost my husband three years ago in an Air Force plane crash. He was a pilot in a F4E jet with an engine problem. My husband flew his plane away from private homes and ejected too late. I was thirty-four at the time." "He died in the Country of Turkey."

"I love the western world and consider myself a western-world-woman." "My late husband loved the world."

"I have a college degree in Computers Communication Management from the University of Maryland. I retired three months ago from the Air Force after fifteen years of service. I will explain later. I retired as a Lieutenant Colonel."

"I also have an arts degree through my military service. My future passion, which I have started, is a great love for fashion design. My favorite cities are in Paris, Washington DC, and New York. The Micas of Design."

"I loved France and Germany and also enjoyed England, Korea and Japan. My daughter was born in Okinawa. She is with extended family by a beautiful lake in the great State of Colorado. She loves to fish and kayak in the summer. She is finding her place in the sun."

"I am a Christian, and I can't imagine life without my Lord. I thank him daily for my many blessings. He is my Rock and Comforter. I have a fear of failure and my Lord has not let me down yet. Nor will he."

"My profile has been carved from the people of the world that I have met. Country and international history I can never get enough of. I crave the information."

"I moved to New York after I retired and now, I am at the crossroads deciding on my future. I have rented an apartment for ninety days. Decisions need to be made soon. Thank you for your time. God Bless You All."

"Alan Arnold Carpenter."

"Let me be frank. I did not become an all-American by myself. I had a coach who believed in me. I had an offensive line that blocked and blocked well for me. Texas had an offensive coordinator who mixed plays up well to confuse the defense."

"I didn't run well against defenses like those of Oklahoma, A and M, Southern Cal and Notre Dame. I ran okay against them, but when you have great days against the Cowboys of Oklahoma State, Kansas and other weaker teams the yards added up. I didn't carry the ball to become an all-American. I carried the ball for Texas to win."

"I learned a lot about myself after I was injured and stopped playing in the latter part of my junior year. I learned that you had to take the knocks with the rocks. You had to take the tackles with the breakaways. Again, I owe my success to the offensive lines over the three years with the Longhorns."

"I became a better man after I was injured. I could finally see the big picture. The young kid who pick-up the yards for Texas after I was hurt; ran hard, ran well and contributed to the team's success."

"It doesn't matter if you are in an office, a bank, or working for a common good; you cannot do it by yourself. The bosses' ideas might work, but they might not as well. Some have to be changed."

"I stand here before you today with this in mind. I want to be a member of your winning team. I don't have to carry the ball; I can be a blocker. If you only believe that a black man can be a winner in athletics, I hope you think again. If you only think that a white man can succeed in business, you need to think that one over too."

"I am ready to serve, do my part and be a team player. None of us can get there alone. I appreciate you all. Thank you."

"Silas Franklyn Fox."

"I have told them almost all of what I have written about thus far. I am happy you are living my story. Please keep reading."

"Savannah Jade Whitlock."

"She repeated much of what I have told you already. She highlighted a few areas of interest. She became tired of teaching school not because of the children and their parents. No, it was the liberal school boards and the idiots who sit on them."

"She was married for only two years. She married a white architect who had designs on moving up by using a back-show-wife as a chance to enhance his position. She told me that he never loved her."

"She mentioned that her parents were getting a divorce because they no longer shared the same direction and plans for the future. She is heartbroken."

"Because of her parent's situation, she decided to move from Livonia and find a position where she could help, create, continue to educate and move forward with success."

"Her presentation was as elegant as she is and from her heart."

Mr. Tate sat back in his chair, sat his glasses on the table, and spoke. "Wow. We have a conference room full of pros."

Mr. Tate told us to take a break for an hour, and then let's talk about what you have heard. We will gather at one o'clock.

The sandwich was tasty but not necessarily what I wanted. I guess I was too interested in what was going to happen next. Barely did we all make it back on time. But we did and Mr. Tate said he was impressed.

"I was impressed." Tate went on to say each of you chose a different path to follow. "It could be said that all roads at times do reach the same destination. Perhaps that's true with these messages we heard."

Mr. Tate asked. "Who has something to say?"

Asia made reference to remarks by Della, Jasper and Alan. "Different but had to be said. Teamwork, it's not who we are but what we stand for and I needed to hear about Wyoming. All good thoughts."

Katarina said, "Asia has gone through hell and has started living again." "That's great to see." Perhaps I hit the nail on the head when thinking out loud that I saw no color but only people in their remarks. Everyone is a class act.

Della's comments were right on. "Some of you told us who you are, while others wanted you to think you knew who we were. I have never heard an All-American like Alan be so upfront and honest. He was very believable."

I made one further comment. Jasper straightened me out on Wyoming.

Savannah added. "I spoke from my heart and it has been aching lately. Others of you spoke with reference to truths and others were on top of their games with their mind. I would hire Asia and Della in a heartbeat."

Again, it was Mr. Tate's turn to remark. "The rest of today I want all of you to interact and to get better acquainted. I am giving you all a day off and invite you to enjoy all what the Resort has to offer tomorrow. We will continue here on Tuesday at eight o'clock on September 11, 2001."

Thirty minutes later, all eight of us gathered and discussed the best way to go about Tate's request. It was decided on Sunday afternoon and one evening session on Sunday we would pair off and have forty-five-minute conversations and a twenty-minute discussion of what topics were discussed.

On Monday morning we would have two more of the pairings and same amount of time for discussion and the follow-up. On Sunday afternoon, these are the discussion pairs. Retired Air Force Asia and the All-American Alan.

Myself and the South Carolina administrator would be one pair. The Osage Native-American and the Michigan elementary teacher would pair. The FBI Agent and the man from Wyoming would make up the sessions. On Sunday evening. Della and Alan. Asia and Savannah. Horatio and Katrina and me and Jasper.

On Monday morning in session three; Della and Horatio. Asia and Katarina. Jasper and I; and Savannah and Alan. The second sessions on Monday included Della and Savannah, Asia and Jasper, Horatio and I and Alan and Katarina.

I will only write of one review heard. The conversation between Asia and Alan. Asia wrote on her profile she had fear of failure. Getting lost and poor direction skills and unintentionally hurting someone. The All-American nailed the answer. "Asia, I was always nervous about going into any ballgame."

"I had to get tackled a couple of times before I felt I was in the game." "I have walked the wrong way out of the River Walk in San Antonio because I was lost. I had been there a dozen times." "Remember how poised you are and how professional you act." "You shoo flies away and never used a swatter." And the kicker! "Relax and live."

On Monday afternoon, we enjoyed many of the features of the Resort. Swimming, putt-putt golf, hiking the grounds and dancing to the jukebox in the inner lounge. We all loved the music of rock-n-roll. One exception from rock. Jasper taught us a couple of line dances. It was a blast.

Monday evening ended with Savannah and I having another one of our talks in the lobby area.

CHAPTER SIX:
CAN YOU BELIEVE IT?

Tuesday, September 11, in St. Petersburg was a beautiful, fall day but still plenty warm. All eight of us were more casually dressed after the break then before when we first began the program.

We were all anxious to get on with it. All eight were at our tables by ten minutes to eight. Mr. Tate joined us about five minutes later dressed in slacks and a sport-shirt, no tie. My thought was that it was time to get down to business.

"Well, how was late Sunday afternoon, evening and Monday?" We all nodded with smiles and he seemed pleased.

Mr. Tate went on to say, "I had a very busy day myself yesterday, and I had two fairly long sessions with the Providers director."

"Our foundation has changed some of our plans because of the quality of you, the candidates."

I looked at my watch and it was eight-forty-five. "I will get into the full details with you as a collectively body and also with you individually." "Before I do, members of my staff are reviewing numbers, positions, leadership and administrative functions."

There was noise outside our door then came the hard knock. "Come in," said Mr. Tate. A member of his staff said, "I am sorry to interrupt, but I am bringing you a television set for there is something tragic happening in New York."

The big television was turned on, volume up and turned to CNN. The pictures on the screen showed people running. In both directions, firemen were running to the first twin tower and some people from the tower were running the opposite direction to safety.

CNN announced that a commercial American Airline Boeing 767 has flown into the tower. The time was eight-forty-six. Everyone in the room was in shock. How could this have happened?

The President of the United States was visiting the Emma E. Booker Elementary School in Sarasota, Florida. CNN showed President Bush being briefed. For a few minutes, the elementary teacher Sandra Kay Daniels continued to read the children's book.

Shortly before nine o'clock, President Bush ordered all commercial jets in the air to be grounded. This also included all private planes.

To our dismay, at nine-oh-three the second plane hit the other tower. A private video filmed from a telephone showed that it was a United Flight another Boeing 767 aircraft.

After the second plane hit the tower, the President boarded Air Force One and the flight began to Offutt Air Force Base in Nebraska. Air Force One landed with fuel almost depleted.

The tragedy did not stop there. At nine-thirty-seven, an American Airlines plane flew into the Pentagon in Virginia. From television pictures, we could see policemen, firefighters, men and women in uniform running and helping others.

After landing at Offutt, the President was taken to an underground bunker in SAC headquarters. Air Force One was also being refueled.

CNN reported a human-interest story that a woman named Lisa Beamer had just talked to her husband on United Flight 93, originally headed for San Francisco had turned around and was headed East. Lisa ended the call to her husband with, "I love you."

In the air, Lisa's husband Todd had gotten a hold of a GTE operator and learned more on the situation. Thirty-two-year-old Todd Beamer and others on that flight would soon become heroes. The GTE operator said, "I heard him say loudly, 'Let's Roll'." And boy did they roll. That flight ended after the plane nose-dived into the ground in Pennsylvania.

It took nearly two and one-half hours to get three thousand, three hundred commercial airliners on the ground. Included in that time were twelve hundred private planes grounded too.

America watched like we did in Florida; tears, cussing, and from the gut statements came from the eight at the tables. America had been attacked on our homeland and the President bunkered down in Nebraska.

At eleven in the morning on September 11, Mr. Tate walked to the front of the room and turned the sound down on the television. He said, "We will pick up from here again at four o'clock this afternoon."

When we resumed five hours later, Mr. Tate was the first to speak. "Three of you eight have spoken to me. I completely understand and I would like the three to tell the group what you have told me."

Katarina Grace Damaris stood at her desk. "My Special FBI Agent Chief Rogers ordered me to cancel my vacation in Florida and return to Seattle by the fastest means possible." She added, "I owe this to my country."

The man from Wyoming, Jasper Levi Crawford stood next. "I have spoken with the foreman and cow-hands on the ranch in Wyoming. And I also spoke with an Army Recruiter in Cheyenne. The Country needs my service and my MOS. I am going back into the Army." Jasper sat down.

I didn't believe my eyes, but then Horatio Geronimo Nightcloud stood. He had tears in his eyes. He said something in his native tongue and cleared his throat." I thought it was an Osage prayer.

"I thought it was time for me to do something else in my life but apparently not."

"I am returning to New Mexico for the US Energy Department needs my math skills and I need to know that I am doing something for my Country."

I thought there would only be three people to stand. I was wrong. Standing was Asia Lynn Dash. "Everyone in this room I want you to stand and stand at attention." We did. "All in this room are proud, loyal and respected Americans." "Especially, the three who stood before me."

"I can't go back into the Air Force because I have retired from service. Alan can't go because of his previous injury and surgeries to his knees. Savannah and Della are not military-experienced and would need to be trained. Silas was a Marine. But told me in our one-on-one he has health issues."

"To the three of you who stood; Katarina, Horatio and Jasper. I am proud to have spent this short time with you. I am proud of you; I salute you and recognize your commitment to America. May our God Bless You and keep you all safe." She then sat down. We all did.

America's President George W. Bush and Air Force One left Offutt at four-thirty to fly back to Washington. Air Force One was escorted by six-American Air Force Jet-Fighters. Air Force One put down in DC at six-forty-four.

Mr. Tate, soon stood. "I knew that this group was special. I will meet you at seven o'clock at the steak restaurant. Tonight's dinner is on me."

It was announced by CNN, CBS, ABC and NBC that the President of the United States would speak to the country at eight-thirty Eastern Time.

I looked at Savannah and spoke. Let's go find a television to watch. America could be at war. We watched for ten minutes.

We went to dinner at seven but I was not ready to eat. I still had something stuck in my throat. Maybe, this proud Marine could return to duty.

After dinner, we were all back in the conference room ready to hear the President's speech. What I took from the President's remarks was this. "They have failed, and we shall overcome."

The last said in the conference room that night was said by Mr. Tate. "We will help the three of you get to when you need to go. The other five we will see you in the morning."

CHAPTER SEVEN:
FIVE CARD DRAW

The five of us all walked to the conference room together. Opening the door, we wondered if we were in the right place.

Instead of eight tables, now there was only five. Mr. Tate's table was taken way in favor of a tall stool. There were two tables that had charting papers lying on them and on-top of the paper were colorful writing pencils and markers.

Our new table assignments had me sitting at table one, Savannah was at two, Asia was in the middle at three, Della was in number four and Alan was at table five.

"Good morning," Mr. Tate said. We all agreed.

"Before I go any further, I will tell you that I have spoken with Katarina, Horatio and Jasper." "Horatio, has accepted a satellite position with us while still working in Albuquerque." "The reason he is not with us this morning is that our company feels that the four children need both a dad and mom around the house."

"I learned more about the man from Chugwater, Wyoming while on the phone. He will be offered a position with the company if he wants it when his Army days are over." "Jasper Levi Crawford, is one hell of man."

"We wanted to hire Katarina. But we know her position on Serving. Being called back by Seattle's highest-ranking agent; sent a strong message to her about her importance to the agency." "I wished her well and said our door is always open to her."

"I will be offering positions to each of you, the remaining five." "I want to begin with Della Faye Sharp. We are offering you a position here in St. Pete as our new Director of Administration. Della, your background is amazing." "You were a unanimous choice."

"Retired Lieutenant Air Force Colonel Asia Lynn Dash, we are offering you a position of Director of International Operations."

"We are offering to Silas, Savannah and Alan position of Associate, International Directors." "The company wants to make the four of you one team; traveling together."

"Asia Dash, you will be the one in charge, giving orders. What your decision is goes. "Any Lieutenant Colonel in the Air Force has done that most of their lives."

"Your salaries and immediate insurance needs will be from the high-end of the national scale. Those will be discussed with you individually."

"For the four of you will have some time here with us. There will be classes on understanding of foreign governments, passport and visa issues, language classes, team functions, staying on American military bases where available and yes; it will be a full schedule."

"Have any of you made the decision?" There were five 'yeses', hugs and handshakes. The family is growing up together. "Nine-eleven has set the tone on a national scale." It is time to kick ass. And I would bet this group can.

"We have worked with our government here at home and you will be traveling on maroon diplomatic government passports. You will be given physicals and plenty of preventive shots before leaving the country. "You will all sign long-term contracts and be given your first paychecks today."

"Now for the next hour, we will take a break."

"One more point of understanding; Della's process will be different than you who will reside normally overseas, coming back here for scheduled breaks and new procedures."

The profile and personalities of the five of us should be recognized. I have lived my story, but during the forty-five-minute periods with the other four I learned a bucket full of new and positive information.

In the Marine Corps, my enlisted friends gave me the nickname of "Sly". Yes, you have heard of a sly fox before. Well, I was called one for nearly six years.

My dad loved major league baseball and was a big fan of the Seattle Mariners. We went to see Edger, Junior and others play many times. When I was growing up, I had several of Griffey's 'gum' cards.

After I graduated from high school and his semester was over at Idaho; my dad and I took a short vacation to Yellowstone National Park. I loved the guizers, the wildlife, and the camping sites but importantly, we had a chance to get to know each other better.

He told me something that has lasted these years. "I will listen to anything that you have to say without criticism, opinion spoken, or correction. I owe that to you." "You, however, must allow me at a later date to respond." I said that would be fair.

On one of the trips to Seattle, we visited Pike's Market and on one of the lower levels, we found a kite and balloon store and we purchased two large kites made in Japan. Now, if Asia was here, she would say, "you told your dad to go fly a kite." Basically, yes. I even laugh at some of Asia's humor.

To conclude this segment, I wanted to tell you that I asked dad to have two of my mother's neck-scarfs. One I wanted to keep to remember; the other I wanted to use as a tail on my kite. My mother flew with me and dad many times.

I wanted to tell you a couple of things that Della spoke to me about. I heard it from her directly, so I guess I can tell you. Della's dad was a corporate defense lawyer with a great history of success. When he became ill for the last time, he officially retired. But his days in court didn't end there. Let me explain.

Within the last few days of his life, he was home in his bed after the doctors said there was nothing more in what they could do. Della said my mother was in the bedroom next door, home with a bad case of the flu. I had been invited home from Charleston to help out; commonly known today as the caregiver.

My mother was asked to be a one-member jury. She came from the second bedroom in her PJ's and a robe. The jury sat in the stuffed chair at the edge of dad's bed.

Della told me that she welcomed the jury and told the lawyer to continue. It was Della's father, the successful lawyer, who said. "I am here to defend death and the transfer of life on earth to eternal life with my God." I was told he said, "You can't rush death, you can't cause death, and you don't know when death will occur."

"Only, our Heavenly father knows that."

The conclusion of this story is very sad, but Della swore it to be the truth. Her dad's last words spoken to anyone were these. "I rest my case and he then closed his eyes." Della told me he had died then.

My conversation with Asia Lynn was sad but very honorable. Lieutenant Colonel Dash, the Wing Public Affairs Officer was assigned to Wright-Pat Air Force Base, in Ohio. Her husband, Air Force Major Jon Dash, had left McDill AFB, Florida on temporary duty overseas at Incirlik, CDI, and Turkey. Many fighter-pilots in Turkey had come down with the serious med-flue. Major Dash, was one of ten pilots who went to Turkey TDY.

Military records plus Wing History explains Major Dash came off the deck in his F4E fighter, soon after take-off, he experienced a pilot's nightmare, the jet had a flameout and with his skills he controlled the plane from the city of Adana, Turkey away from the population center. He was late in ejecting and died when his shoot didn't open all of the way. He was killed instantly.

Major Dash, was an honor Graduate from the United States Air Force Academy, near Colorado Springs. He will be buried on the Academy

Grounds in the "Honors" cemetery. The flag was flown there at half-staff for one week. He is buried on the knoll of the hill overlooking the Flag Poles.

Asia Lynn went to Dover Air Force Base and after official arrival ceremonies at Dover continued the journey to Colorado Springs by commercial air.

The United Pilot said, "Ladies and Gentlemen, we are flying home to Colorado Springs an American Air Force hero. An Air Force Officer-pilot who was killed in the line of duty while overseas. Also, aboard this flight, is his wife; an Air Force Lieutenant Colonel. Please show respect.

A man seated in First Class walked up to the front of the cabin and talked to the Steward aboard the flight. Within a few seconds, the man who identified himself as a retired Bird Colonel in the Air Force spoke to the aircraft's passengers.

"I would like anyone of you on board, who know the words to join in with me as we sing." My eyes have seen the glory of the coming of the Lord, etc. etc., and nearly another forty voices from the front of the cabin to the back of the plane were singing."

"Glory, glory Hallelujah; glory, glory Hallelujah; glory, glory Hallelujah, his truth is marching on." Asia said his voice was a beautiful second tenor. Asia said she couldn't help but cry.

LATER WHEN THE TIDE COMES IN | 55

Asia also said that the gentleman seated across the aisle from her said. "This is really Air Force One."

Asia Lynn was the first off the airplane and was taken down to the unloading of her husband's body. She joined the Honor Color Guard from the Academy. They were sharp, précised, dazzled those watching and performed with the understanding of the family and the country's gratitude for his service.

He was placed in the hearse, given the slow precision salute, then slowly driven away. Asia Lynn was slowly driven away in a blue Air Force sedan with the American flag flying proudly. "Aim High...Fly. Fight. Win." Some don't come home that way.

Then the plane unloaded. Not one dry eye.

One thing I forgot to tell you about Asia is when she was a First Lieutenant, she was pictured in many US Air Force Recruitment Posters. She was recognized then as special. She was seen across America in Class "A" Blues. In my opinion; she was not a fifteen-oh-five-type. Air Force people will know what I am writing about.

Savannah Jade and I didn't have a visiting forty-five minutes together; but talked to each other for several hours at different times. I will make these comments very short. Savannah asked, "Can we be a couple?" My response to her was, "I don't think so."

I was deeply impressed with the conversation I had with Alan Carpenter. We didn't talk about pro or college sports. No, he was more interested in where I grew up because he said he had heard so much about the Pacific Northwest.

I did ask him why with all of the great schools in the country did he chose to go to University of Texas. His answer was right on. "I have the love for my State of Texas as you do for the State of Washington."

"After coming to Florida," Alan said, "There are three places I would like to tour and visit. Colorado, Wyoming, and Washington." "I want to have the famous chili in Chugwater, Wyoming." Delicious, I said. "Seafood at Invers in Seattle," that's outstanding, I told him. And a baseball game at Coors Field in Denver." I told him I was with him on the Chili and the seafood, but I'll watch my baseball in Seattle.

The hour's break was over and we were all back in our seats.

Mr. Tate standing next to his stool said, "I've been busy this hour, no break but conversation with my two bosses." "In the conversation, I listened as I was told we needed to rewrite some of the company's mission statements. I would be given drafts of the statements mid-morning tomorrow."

"Yes, he said, "We will have a national version and also an international version to start with; and finally, a version that defines us as one mission, one direction, and one position that represents who we are. I am excited about this."

Della Faye Sharp asked. "What can we do to help?" The answer floored me. Mr. Tate said, "the five of your will co-author our mission of the future. We want to hear what your thoughts are and why. The company will make the final decision, but your thoughts will be heard."

Mr. Tate said, "Let's go get a snack and be adjourned until tomorrow morning at eight o'clock." I was all in favor of that.

I had a hard time resting last evening and certainly sleeping during the night, for I believe what Providers is doing in reference the mission statement is all wrong.

Many believe that a mission statement describes what your company does. Also believing describing how your company does what it does and lastly, why does the company do what it does?

In my opinion, Providers don't need a mission statement but a vision statement. In my mind, a vision statement focuses on tomorrow. A mission statement is what the company does today. With the growth coming to Providers their vision is going to happen in the near future; tomorrow.

In my view, a plan, action and success allow to the vision to be seen and growth to continue. I think in a nutshell, I think Providers should practice sustainable development Internationally. Finally, the vision statement motivates your staff and inspires others. The mission statement is telling what you are trying to do and what you ought to do.

At eight-twenty this morning, at our first session of the day; I presented this theory to Mr. Tate. He commented, "What I like about this group of people is that before they get to read the company's drafts, the five of you are strong enough to state your thinking and present your opinions."

"Thank you for that."

Mr. Tate excused himself from the group and said, "Sit here and give me ten- minutes." It took Mr. Tate about twenty minutes before he came back.

He was not alone, with him were distinguished looking men in their late fifties. Mr. Tate introduced them to us as the Company President, Robert W. Williamson, and the Chief Operating Officer, Sedgwick K. Carlson.

Each of them came by our tables and shook hands with each of us.

Mr. Williamson asked, "Silas what kind of background do you have to have made the point to Blake about the mission statement?" I started to speak, when he interrupted me and said, "we hear you loud and clear."

As they say in a double's tennis match, the ball is now in our court. Mr. Carlson broke the silence, "how long would it take for the five of your minds to write a vision statement? Would we see a draft today?"

The US Air Force Lt. Colonel retired answered, "Yes, before the day is over." I wondered if Asia Lynn had a mouse in her pocket or not. She was more than positive.

All five of us had written statements before, but not since college courses and never for a corporation. By the way, Asia's believing in me raised her standard to above one-hundred percent.

When the company's big guys left, Blake Tate asked, "is this a kettle of fish or are the sharks coming out?"

Mr. Tate said, "I will see you all in about three hours."

Savannah was the last to convince of a vision plan in the group. She was now on board. "I like things short and sweet," Della said. "So do I," Savannah remarked.

I asked if I could start with a line we could built on? "What's the line?" Alan asked.

PROVIDERS' VISION – Achieving International Care and Education through Sustainable Development, Individual Proficiency, with Corporate Determined Structure and Human Energy.

One hour early, we sent word to Mr. Tate we had a vision statement prepared. We felt comfortable with our efforts. Two hours later we found out the statement would be recommended for use internationally.

When Mr. Tate settled down, and found his stool again, he said, "I think it is time that I tell you the company's story."

"The two men you were introduced to; Williamson and Carlson started this company thirty-one-years-ago in Portsmouth, Ohio. They were best friends and ball playing buddies in high school and have stayed friends in business for all these years."

"The company was originally named PROVIDERS – MANKIND; and twenty-five years ago was changed to the current name. Fifteen years ago, the company moved from Portsmouth to Fort Myers, Florida and in 1992 moved here to Saint Pete."

"I have been with the company nearly ten-years and joined them after several years with the American Red Cross. Similar services but different processes. I'll will get into that later."

"Currently, after hiring the five of you; we have fifty-one people employed. Eighteen here in Pete, four on the road in country; mostly fundraisers and those overseas. Twenty-three of the employees have minorities backgrounds, and we have hired people from several-English-speaking nations."

"We have different international teams of all white, all black, all Latinos, and all Orientals. You are the first mix-racial team we have put together. Twenty-eight people are currently in eight countries. We have services now in Peru, Kosovo, Portugal, Bahrain, Netherlands, Belgium, Turkey and Italy."

"We on purpose, will not tell the public where we are serving. We think, "They don't need to know." "Another secret or private information is that we have Global Security, in which we pay for from others." "When you get ready for travel, we will inform you well of the security you will have where you will be going first."

"Also, Horatio has already been given his first assignment. Numbers are very important to us as are percentages, ages, incomes, and a whole lot more."

"After we establish that the four of you are ready to go; prepared, schooled and completely ready, you will receive a crash-three-week course of the language of the country assigned."

"I want to make one thing perfectly clear. There are countries that will not allow international different or racially different couples to come into their countries. We hired the four or the traveling team as individuals and not as pairs. If that changes, you would still travel together as two blacks and two whites." "We think that will work."

"In all honesty, even with your backgrounds, talents, integrity, pride, and purpose; all of you have so much to learn in a very short period of time. There is a major reason why we give such a difficult exam when you apply for you to prove that you are ready for the challenge."

If it turns out that one of you is a little slow on the pick-up, we will not make team changes. No, we will tutor, and delay until all are completely prepared." "Now, that is the least of my worries."

"I told you the difference between the American Red Cross and us. The Red Cross is worked with donations. We also work with donations but also government grants."

"Our government requires us to inform it of who is going and where plus the information on length of time expected and duties to be performed." "Even when the foreign government doesn't like the United States; they like the work and the programs we do in their country."

"Here are some of the reasons why we go: typhoons, hurricanes, monsoons, flooding, dams breaking, and many social injustice trips." "You all recognize the emergency issues, but others we will deal with on a one on team discussion. Much of what we do is on a 'hush' but 'trusted' path of development and equal gains. The home team has to be further ahead when we leave than when we got there." "More on this to come."

"Now. If you went to an English-speaking country, you could be ready to go sooner than you think. Language barriers are 'big' to overcome. Therefore, if you are given a location where languages are an issue, be expecting at least a second trip to the same country at another location."

"Example, if you are in Northern Italy on the first trip and in Southern Italy on the second trip; yes, both are in Italy but two completely different locations and experiences." "Same with Greece, Turkey, Iran, Syria, etc." "My job is to get you ready."

"You will never be sent to a war zone or what is called a 'hot spot'." "Your safety is our biggest concern. The country where you are headed is well aware of your coming. They will keep you safe and secure."

"Does anyone one of you want to leave and forget it?" Alan answered, "Hell no!"

Mr. Tate said, "Let's break for today, and tomorrow we will set a schedule for you to go and return and tomorrow will start the explanation of what is required and expected. See you at eight in the morning."

Yes, looking at Asia, Savannah, Alan and the mirror of myself, we are fired up.

CHAPTER EIGHT:
IT'S HARD TO BELIEVE

Mr. Tate brought up a very good point. "Since the airlines say that it will be still another three days before they get back on schedule, let's plan to have you leave on the Seventeenth and on the Second of October, you are back here for the official start of your training and preparation. That will give us three more days to work now."

He asked if there are any questions. I think we all raised on hand simultaneously.

"Let's start in the middle of the table then, Asia what is your question?" "Will you have us do any project or work during those two weeks?"

"No." he said.

'Della, your question." Mr. Take will the company help us schedule our flights?" "Yes, we will get your itineraries and do that tomorrow." "Savannah, a question from you." "Sir, will the flights be at our cost?" "I will see if we can cover those costs."

"Okay, gentlemen; Alan you go first." "Mr. Tate, where will we stay during the training time here in Saint Pete?" His response surprised us. "The company has corporate living spaces and each of you will stay there. Meals will be included." "What does the Sly Fox have to ask?" "What would you like us to wear during the training?" "Pure casual." He spoke.

"All you have to do is be here on time. We will have everything provided for your training."

"Mr. Tate." Asia Lynn spoke. "Do you have a clue yet as to where our first training will be for what location and when will we know that?" "That question has been asked to upper management." I think we are looking for three possible locations." "Soul, South Korea, Madrid, Spain or Athens, Greece." 'We would be staying in one of those cities, working however, a few miles outside the city." "I might know the final answer, before you leave for home."

"Tomorrow morning, we will take new passport pictures in casual clothes." "Following, we will have one of our administration folks walk you through the government paperwork." "It should take about an hour each."

"Where ever you are going, we will be starting with their language training." "You will be trained by one with the same native tongue who has English as a second language." "That, by the way, hastens the training time." "We will be speaking some of that language during the second part of the training period."

"Don't panic, you will get through it."

"That brings up another talking point." "I know that we won't grasp all of the languages immediately. Any one of you could be the quickest, but we are also expecting each of you to be prepared for off-time tutoring of your fellow-team member when and if it is required." "Remember, we don't change team members, we wait until all are prepared."

"You all will see a video of the point-of-contact of where you are going and that person will address you on customs, landing instructions, diets, and everything under the sun. You will have about five total videos and will see each multiple times."

"When we talk about a Country, there is a quick overview of the Country considered. Where is it located and how does it act toward the United States and is it a Western or Eastern Country?"

"When we are considering South Korea, Spain and Greece, we must realize there are differences in the make-up of each Country. For instance, after the Korean War in the early 1950's, the South Korean Country took on a look similar to the United States with its Executive, Legislative and Judicial Branches of Government."

"However, South Korea has a President elected by the people, it doesn't have a Vice President, but a Prime Minister selected by its Parliament."

"There is a similar process in Greece, where every five years the Parliament of Greece selects and elects the President. Greece holds other elections every four years to elect other positions within its government. Greece has an Executive Branch, Legislative Branch and Judiciary."

"The Central Government of Spain has an Executive Branch and what it calls the General State Administration of the Kingdom of Spain. The system works under a Parliament known as the General Courts."

"In Spain there is a ruling Monarch, who serves as the Head of State." "The Prime Minister of Spain acts like a President of any other Country."

"These facts are not complete and only point out the differences between countries. When a country has been selected to achieve some work there; then we go into depth about how the government works and what steps we must take to be allowed in and for how long and what are we going to achieve while there."

"Sometimes it gets really crazy and we back out of the proposed commitment until a later date. In the past, we have successes in the countries reviewed."

"We are not going to go through the process and completing the forms for passports and visas. The reason the three of you who have passports must turn those in when we request an up-date or new issue."

"It seems crazy that Asia doesn't have a passport but has been traveling on the Military Orders as the document of record. The other three of you have different lengths of time left on the passport and therefore, only one of you have had the passport that our company travels on."

"When you return in October, please bring your active passport back with you."

"Now, who is ready for lunch?" "We will continue at one," Mr. Tate said.

When we returned on time from lunch, I asked Mr. Tate did the company had a "Code of Ethics"?

"I was going to bring that topic up latter, but we will do it now."

"The PROVIDERS CODE OF ETHICS: Respect the individual, company or country. Act with direction, strive for excellence and always do the right thing. Obey all laws in every land we enter. Serve others like we would like to be served."

"Naturally, we live with diversity and our belief of anti-discrimination."

"Since we are doing this now, the company also has a CODE OF CONDUCT."

"PROVIDERS CODE OF CONDUCT: Written by Senior, Executive Management. Available to all employees."

"Eliminate all harassment and corruption. Following the Corporate Rules is our way of doing business. Never be involved with conflicts of interest. Secure company assets. Support each other at all times."

"We live by these two codes." "Thanks for bring up the topic of ethics."

"You four are sharp as tacks, thinkers, quick on your feet and far ahead of most of our previous hirers. Therefore, I will add at least one more company input; our Corporate Strategy."

"As we grow together, you will learn and hear much more than what I will tell you today. It is truly required that you know what Corporate does. Understand the risks and the rewards. We always require employees to sharpen their skills when performing any of our functions."

"You will all be engaged in better execution of duties. Example: If you get your projects done when overseas before schedule; you will have saved the company thousands of dollars to be used elsewhere."

"You will hear us talk about aligning planning and execution."

"Our theory, in a nutshell, is to see it before it happens, understand how it happens, and make it happen."

"That is why we are the best in the world for what we do; and why the countries of the world want us to do what we do, and we do what we always do because we are prepared for what we do." "Our success is not by luck, but by great hiring practices, excellent planning, and nearly flawless execution."

"I have talked too much today." Mr. Tate said, "Now you tell me something."

Savannah and I would love to bring you up to date Mr. Tate, but privately. "Okay, then let's take an hour's break and you two come with me."

Walking down one of the corporate hallways and into Blake Tate's office. It is how I could imagine it at the White House in DC. First-class and not much left for anyone's imagination.

We were seated and Mr. Tate got right to the point of the visit. "Are you going to tell me something that will complicate the mission?"

Savannah was the first to speak. "No Sir, just the opposite. We have both come to realize that in college, we were both kids, adults today. Then there was a sensation of fascination, not realization, lack of motivation, and youthful juices flowing." "The two of us could be friends, but as adults are lives have changed completely. My teaching experiences and his time in the Marine Corps were periods of education far different than university learning."

I jumped in then and spoke. Savannah and I were very close when we in college at Idaho. That has all changed. We have had many discussions since being here and realize that we have both grown-ups. I have great respect for Savannah, but there is no longer any consideration for romance.

Savannah chimed in again. "In high school in Detroit, a white young man was hard to find in the city. Anyway, the kind you would like to take home and meet mom. Young, at Idaho, I was in total awe at the number in every class and throughout the college."

I jumped in to add. At Dewey Junior High, you could count the black kids on both of my hands. At Moscow High School, I believe there were four in total.

"Mr. Tate, when I brought home the white architect, my mother had a fit. She said that I would be rowing the boat up-river if I got married to him. She was right."

I added that Savannah and I have had no encounters that anyone would object too. It has been with mature thinking that will make us better individual employees. We were both struck on your comments several days ago as being hired as individuals.

We are different today than seven or eight years ago, and the Lord knows that I did grow up when in the Marine Corps. Also, while in the Corps I worked for one black female NCO and one white female Officer with great success.

I see absolutely no reason whatsoever that we couldn't both work for Asia Lynn Dash. Her demeanor was much like the Captain I served under part of my time in the Corps. Asia is one of the retired 'pros' from the Air Force.

Mr. Tate smiled at both of us. He shook our hands and said, "Thank you both." "Let's go back and join the others." I am glad visit is over.

When returning to the others, Mr. Tate asked. "Would either of the two of you like a private conversation with me." There were no takers.

The rest of the afternoon was for each of us to spend time with Mr. Tate and a financial officer going through salary, insurance and direct deposit information.

The medium salary range in 2001 was forty-two thousand, two-hundred and twenty-two dollars. I accepted a salary of fifty-six thousand five hundred dollars.

I would be paid four-thousand, seven hundred and three dollars per month. Approximately twenty-two twenty every two weeks. The company also paid for one-hundred-thousand-dollars' worth of life insurance and health insurance. I was pleased with that.

Tomorrow, Mr. Tate said, "We will finish up before you head for your two-week break." "Remember, the Second of October is just around the corner."

When we left the tables, Asia winked at me. Oh well, life goes on.

When we arrived for the opening of the last official day in Florida before our break. We were surprised to see Misters Williamson and Carlson already in place.

Mr. Tate said, "These gentlemen have an announcement to be made." "Mr. Williamson."

We were going to hear some words of wisdom from the President of the Company. I hope I am prepared for this.

Mr. Williamson began. "I doubt if we have had the quality of all eight original candidates than what you all represented." "We are happy and excited about the five of the group taking positions of importance within the organization. Della will be a 'super-star' in the front office. The administrative chores will rest with her and her alone in the near future."

"We believe deeply in the four of you and are wanting to expand our company's level of excellence by adding one word to duties. That word is diplomacy. The word will affect all four of you. Your reasoning capacity is exceptional. In the past, the two of us made major decisions without knowing all of the facts and all of them haven't panned out for the good."

"Therefore, when you return on the Second of October; the four of you will spend one week's time with us on company diplomacy before the Spanish Language course will begin. Folks, your first assignment will be in Spain and it will include our company's policy on European services that PROVIDERS will offer in the future."

"Don't be surprised if the trip to Spain and meeting with government officials will set the pattern of the future with up-dates for France, Germany, Italy, Greece, Turkey and even Iran."

"We have a former Air Force Public Affairs Officer, in Asia Lynn. We have a talented, educated teacher in Savannah Jade, we have from a previous position of "corporate spokesman" Alan Arnold, and finally, a formerly professional Marine who won over a dozen public speaking titles in high school and college and set the University of Idaho's record of nineteen debate wins."

"When we present to the different governments in each presentation, we will have four presenters representing our mission, our integrity, our world's position and added information. "

Mr. Carlson added. "We have others who can serve and represent us in the field; but you four will be in the limelight in the country's capitals." "We believe this is the best way to go with the four of you. It is your presents of dignity, charm, intelligence and functional organizations goals, which allows us the success we expect."

"Comments?" I knew Asia Lynn would jump all over this. "I can see where public affairs can certainly be translated to corporate or governmental affairs." "I love the concept."

"The soft-spoken Alan with a vocabulary longer than the Mississippi River responded with this. "We are at your service to enhance your position worldwide."

Savannah Jade added, "Our diversities, our presentations, our desire to achieve as individuals and as a team of quality Americans, I guarantee, will increase acceptance and credibility instantly."

I was the last to speak. "I will always be a part of the few but proud Marines. I will help translate that from the Corps to our team and to the representatives of other countries. I will proudly represent the company and help move forward to increase the service and dedication to others. You made us all proud."

The distinguished gentlemen left leaving Mr. Tate to speak. "Furthermore, the company when you return in October, will take each of you to tailors for making a new wardrobe for all of you. No costs from your pockets."

"Before we leave here this morning, I wanted to speak for a moment on the 'City of Churches' here in St. Pete. In St. Pete and the nearby communities, there are ninety-two churches of every denomination you could think of."

"I bring this up because seven-mega churches in St. Pete have approached us in the past asking for our help in working in areas where they have done international projects in various places that make conditions for those people much better."

"We are always touched when they ask us for help. We might have additional requests when you all return."

Savannah asked Mr. Tate a question. "Are you married?" "Thank you for the question he said."

"I was once. I worked for the Mile High Chapter of the American Red Cross in Denver. My wife Julie was a school counselor at Columbine High School."

"She had worked with the two shooters. We were both good friends of Dave Sanders and his wife. She worked very closely with those killed and many students after the tragedy."

"Three years later, she had passed. Records said it was a suicide. I think she only made a tragic mistake." I worked at the Red Cross for two more years before coming here."

Mr. Tate said, "Let's go get you packed and prepaid for the trip to the airport in Tampa Bay." We all stood, hugged each other, shook hands and smiled from ear to ear. My dad is going to be impressed.

CHAPTER NINE:
ANSWERING THE CALLS TO SEABECK

I realized that life takes us to unexpected places, but love brings us home. Well, here I am. It has been a while, but I am back. I checked into and got keys to the apartment.

After visiting the restroom and looking into the mirror; I headed out the front door, down past the General Store and out to the end of the dock. I loved the smell of the water and the breeze of the air filling my lungs again and again.

In Seabeck, I listened to some of my music for the sounds of the past. Johnny Cash sang, "I wear the black for the poor and the beaten down. I wear the black for the people who never read; or listened to the words that Jesus said." "I wear the black for the sickly and lonely old. Until things are brighter in the world, I'm the man in black." Dad played this song over and over again.

I looked out my window and watched the seagulls, the birds of the sea, soaring and diving through the windy air and below; the cool, fresh, still water.

When Johnny Cash sang, most lyrics were about American folks; but he knew what it was like worldwide. When Cash and June Carter went to Vietnam, they sang for all two-hundred and twenty-five thousand. They loved every GI in country. When Cash wrote and recorded that music in 1971, it was still current and fit for 2001 from thirty years later.

The next song by Cash I played was, "What is Truth?" One lyric of that song that I will always remember is, "and the voice of youth cried out; what is truth?" There were thousands of American youths, wearing uniforms and jungle boots, in Vietnam wanting to know what is truth?

My mind was racing a little, but I thought what I had just experienced in Saint Petersburg what Providers, the company, is doing throughout the parts of the world. Improving living conditions, trying to improve the lives of thousands, providing training for so many, and teaching ways for people to stand on their own two feet.

Providers know truth through diplomacy and is learning how to transmit the information worldwide through one country, one city, one location at a time. Sometimes, only one person at a time is what's available to them.

Trout were jumping for the flies just above the water, and my mind was saying out loud: Providers are teaching truth to the world. One person at a time, one after another. And I am going to be a part of that.

I was a little startled when the phone rang for the second ring. Hello, this is Silas. "What is going on in the other side of the country?" Yes, it was Asia Lynn. I have been listening to music and letting my mind wonder a little. How about you?

"You are the only one that I am calling, but I tell you, I am a little excited about the prospects of the future with a person like you and a company like Providers. Do you think we can make a difference?" I said, absolutely, no doubt about it.

Asia said. "Stay safe, enjoy your free time and call me." Now that was an invitation that soon I would have to follow up on. Day three at home and I have heard from the International Director. No! That was my friend Asia.

After I got off the phone with Asia Lynn, I went through my notes and found the phone numbers of Horatio in New Mexico and Jasper in Wyoming. I wanted to see how Horatio and family were doing and I wanted to personally thank Jasper for his service to his country and what a pleasure it was to meet him.

I called Horatio. He answered the phone by saying, "Silas, how are you?" I am fine, how about you and your family? "Well, I guess you have heard already that my wife Priscilla and myself will be coming to Florida in early October to teach the four of you 'real' Spanish of Spain.

"You will hear first-hand from the woman who taught me the language so well. When we get done in about one week you will be able to confer with the Parliament, order food on the street, and barter for anything you want in the city." "You won't receive any of the American teaching high school or college 'Spanish' pushed in our country today."

I asked how did all of this come about? "Providers called, asked; I had more vacation time: Priscilla and I jumped at the time and accepted the challenge." Is it going to be a challenge with the four of us?

"No, not really. Savannah, who has had Spanish in high school and college and who has learned the Mexican junk will have to learn new tones, emphasis on some words and the street verbiage of Madrid and Barcelona. I think she can and do it quickly."

Can you give myself and Asia a head start? "I could fax you a copy of two-hundred and fifty keywords and phrases and translations later today." Can I pass them along to Asia? "Oh, I would love you to do that."

What about the company you work for; how are they treating this now? "They are willing to get from me what they can and they know that I am only a phone call away for an emergency."

Do you have time for another couple of questions? "Shoot." How are the kids doing? "The two oldest are teenagers; does that answer your question?" "The younger two are 'cool', learning and watching their older brother and sister in trying to find out, what works and what doesn't." "My wife and I are too sharp for those not yet pros."

My brother, can I inform Asia and let us start on your fax? "Sure, but be surprised when we show us. It is my understanding that you will only be doing the 'diplomacy' thing for a couple of days and not a week as stated. My wife and I will be on their heels ready to move in."

It took me to the fifth call before I reached the cowboy from Chugwater. When he answered the phone, I heard talking in the background. "My girl-friend and her parents are here and we are talking about a hurried wedding." Jasper spoke.

Are you serious, I asked? "The most serious I have been in years. I have already gotten my assignment from the Army and it will be a teaching position for three years. Janet, from Cheyenne, was someone that I did not want to lose."

"The Army know that I am coming accompanied. The wedding will be done in a

Christian Church in Cheyenne two weeks from Saturday. Ironically, the one doing the ceremony is a former retired, Army Chaplain. He helped put this together for us."

Was this in the cards when I saw you in Florida? "Yes, but it was pushed to the front of the line after nine-eleven hit." "I wish you guys could come." Is that an official invitation? "Yes." What time of day will it be? "Eight o'clock in the evening." What will the uniform of the day be? "Wyoming casual." I wrote on October 15, 2001, First Christian Church, Cheyenne, Wyoming. I too, have a date book for recorded thoughts.

Asia Lynn answered the phone after the third-ring. "Hello, Silas." She spoke. "I was hoping you would call." Do you have a few minutes? "All the time that you want."

Boy, do I have news for you. "Good, I hope." Absolutely. Let me begin with Horatio's phone call. He and his wife are coming to Florida to do our language class on Spanish. "How do you know this?" He let the cat out of the bag when I called.

We are going to learn the language of Spain. Real Spanish.

Now, I would like to ask you a personal question. How would you like to spend some money and fly to Wyoming on October 15 and back to Florida on Sunday, October 16? "Why?"

Jasper and Janet are getting married at the First Christian Church in Cheyenne at eight o'clock Wyoming time on October fifteenth. Do you think you and I could swing it? "I would love it." Asia replied.

I don't know where the time went but Asia and I talked for over an hour. I can't remember many of the topics. But I do remember one. Asia wants to fly to Seattle and see the Northwest before we head to Florida for our next session on October Second. I told her I had a second bedroom in my apartment in Seabeck.

The phone rang again in about twenty minutes. "I want to see what you are like in a slowed-down environment like on Puget Sound." Do you like to fish? I asked her? "I don't know, I never have myself. That's my daughter's second favorite thing to do." "Eating fish is not my favorite menu." She added.

"I hope you don't mind; I will be at the Seattle-Tacoma Airport at eleven-twenty in the morning the day after tomorrow. I'm flying Alaska Airlines." Mind? I'm excited. I told her. Pack for Florida, but be casual for here, I told her. This isn't New York. "Neither am I," she replied.

CHAPTER TEN:
HELLO SEA-TAC

My car is not new and shiny, but very reliable. I left Seabeck, made my way toward Bremerton, through Bremerton past Gorst, Port Orchard, Gig Harbor, crossed the Tacoma's Narrows Bridge left Highway Sixteen and into Tacoma hit Interstate Five and started the nineteen miles to Sea-Tac.

It is easy to get off at the Seattle-Tacoma Airport exit from Interstate Five but getting into one of the parking garages takes thinking, courage and a memory to remember the garage number, floor number and spot number and which elevator.

I was smart, I had been here before; I would be excited having Asia with me, so I wrote every number and location down on a yellow-sticky note pac. The Alaska Airlines area was the largest at the airport but the easy to get to and through.

I looked at my watch and it was still twenty-five minutes before she was due to arrive. There was still a distance to walk, but I had a little time to spare. I thought about getting flowers, but I said no. But on my second choice, I said yes. Washington State Chocolates. A nice two-pound box. When I got there, I changed my mind.

Instead of chocolates a box of Washington Applets and Cottlets. I loved em'.

Now to the gate and the new security process on arrivals. Basically, the same as before, but with a little bit more distance between. This was the greatest Chamber of Commerce Day the City of Seattle had in months. Bright sunshine, smooth water and absolutely no rain.

She was waving; she saw me first. I hugged her first and quite tightly. She made it here safe and sound and was dressed in complete comfortable clothes with a light-wind-breaker in her arms along with her purse. I volunteered to carry her goodies and handed her the small package. She said, "What is this?" Something good, I said.

We needed a porter and his wagon when we got to the luggage area. I got my note card out of my pocket and handed it to the porter. "Please follow me," he said. Wow! He took me right to the car and I gave him a nice tip. "Thank you."

I helped Asia into the passenger seat, made her buckle up and went to the driver's side from behind the car. I kept my billfold out of my pants, and headed down the circle drive to pay the fee and headed out to Interstate Five.

My first major question to her was to Seattle to the ferry or drive around to the end of the sound to home? I knew what she would say. "To Seattle and the ferry to Bremerton." We were off and running both wearing smiles with our dark-glasses.

When she saw the Boeing Commercial Aircraft at Renton, she said. "Wow!" "What a beautiful day." I lied when I said, just typical for Seattle.

We got to the Coleman Docks we had thirty minutes before the ferry would dock. We are waiting for the ferry named Nisqually.

Are you hungry or do you want to wait and eat in Bremerton at the Noah Ark Restaurant? "I'll wait," She replied.

"We are headed to your early life stomping grounds," Yes, I said, it will always be my real home. There is something about the Sound.

There were two toots. The ferry is about to dock. The cars rolled off and it was our time to get on. From the car we walked a short distance to the steps leading upstairs and into the bright sunshine from the outdoors. Do you want to sit in here or head to the outdoors? She didn't answer, she just headed to the doorways.

It is fun to go to the very front of the ferry and stand and watch both the car deck and the sites on the water and shoreline. She looked at me and said, "I love it."

There was just a little chatter for the next fifty minutes and soon it was time to head back to the car. She looked at Bainbridge Island, Waterman, Annapolis and Port Orchard as the Nisqually made his way to dock and tie up. We drove slowly off the ferry and onto the somewhat quiet streets of Bremerton.

We both had rib eyes, baked potatoes, salad and vegetables at Noah's. She loved it. Anyway, she said she did. When we left the restaurant, it was twenty-after four. We will be home about six; a half hour or so before dark.

She couldn't believe my story until she saw my little Chapel at Lonerock. "This is beautiful she said. I don't need New York, the people or the noise." It was about fifteen-minutes from Lonerock to the apartment in Seabeck. "When you said on the water of Puget Sound; you were not kidding."

Unloading the car was not a chore but a lesson for me. "Two of the suitcases, I will not need to get into. This one and that bag is all." "She came into the living room from the bathroom all smiles. Can we see the sun-set over the Cascades?" She spoke. Out the front door we went.

Can you remember the old song lyrics, "the fish are jumping and the sky is so high?" Yep, you guessed it. Live entertaining on the Sound and you didn't have to pay for it.

About eight o'clock she said. "My day is done and I have to crash." I walked her to her bedroom door. She smiled and this time she hugged me tightly. The last thing she said before she shut her door was this. "Do we get to fish tomorrow?" Later when the tide comes in.

In the morning, we went to Swedes for bagels and coffee. I told Asia that she didn't have to answer my next question, but I did have to ask. You are thirty-seven-years-of age, right? You have a four-year college degree and you just retired from the Air Force. How?

"I have a full-salary retirement from the Air Force because of a botched surgery by an Air Force doctor. This was just a little over a year ago. About six or seven months ago, the Air Force asked if I wanted a settlement or an early retirement. I chose early retirement. I served on active duty for just over fifteen years."

"I will answer your follow-up question. Yes, I am fine because of a second surgery from a civilian specialist surgeon who changed my entire life. He fixed the problem and I am in very good health. There is nothing I can't do concerning physical activities."

"Would you like to know more?" No, I was a little perplexed and I wanted to hear you in person say that all is well. I believe in you, happy to work with and for you, and have relaxed some after your answers. "How about you." She questioned.

I have Marine Corps knees. I felt at times my physical training in the Corps was a little too much. I never complained or mentioned this once on active duty. I never played real competitive sports in high school or college.

Years ago, my knees would swell just after some neighborhood games. When in the Corps, I soaked knees on many of nights.

I am in my early thirties, does my age bother you for any reason? "No, a female is expected to outlive a male by some six years. That makes us even." She spoke with a smile.

Asia Lynn, I have to ask another question. What would you like to do while we are here? "That's really up to you," After spending a couple of days here, would you like to take an all-day drive to Moscow and visit my dad? "Yes, of course."

It is about a seven-hour drive from here and we could site-see along the way. I want to leave my car with my dad and we can fly out to Florida from Spokane through Chicago.

"I have a question for you. When do we get to fish?" Later, when the tide comes in. Between five and dark, the fishing should be good. If we catch something we will throw it back in the Sound.

There was a sandwich shop inside the little store, across the street from the Conference

Grounds. Should we see the grounds, walk the docks and then have lunch? "Sounds great to me."

Did you bring another jacket that is a little warmer? If not, I have something you can wear. She finished her second cup of coffee and we headed to the door and the car.

On the way home, we went by the little 'office' store and picked up Horatio's fax. We had them also make a couple of copies for us. Let's table this until we get to my dad's.

I told the gentlemen at the apartment office that I wasn't expecting a refund but I would be leaving about one week early. That is more than good he said.

The Conference Grounds in Seabeck, date back to the late forties I have been told. The bridge over the lagoon wasn't very pretty now; water will come in when the tide arrives.

I am so glad you are here I said.

Walking out the full-length of the dock and see the fishing and pleasure boats was a new experience for the Grand Junction, Colorado woman. I asked her another question as we walked. What makes you a western-world-woman more or less than a woman in the west?

"Perhaps, that is your best question of the day." Well, do you have an answer? "Not at this time."

"But when I do, you will be the first to know."

Sandwiches in Seabeck are not too exotic. Peanut butter and jelly, tuna fish and toasted cheese. "Do you have tomato soup," she asked?" The man answered yes. "I will have a tomato soup and toasted cheese with a sugar-free coke." Make that two, please.

Both the sandwiches and soup were hot. We continued to laugh, smile and enjoy each other's company.

Heading back to the car, I spoke softly and asked if another question would be alright. "Yes, go." Could you tell me a little bit about your daughter? "Yes, but at a time in the future where and when it will be more comfortable for both of us."

I had one last question that was burning in my mind. How about one more question. "Fire way when you are ready."

How long do you expect to wait before you would ever be ready or willing for marriage? "I'm glad that you have asked that question, I have a prepared answer. I am sure that it will probably take about five or six years. Part of this answer will be given to you when I talk to you about my daughter."

"Silas, you must realize that if I didn't feel as comfortable as I do with you. My trust and comforts with you are high and off the charts. It I didn't feel this way; there would be no way in hell that I would be here in this little village of Seabeck with a man that I ran into in a hotel lounge in Florida only a few weeks ago."

"I knew in my heart of hearts that I would be safe and protected, cared for and appreciated. I knew that I had no worries about coming here on a visit to see a little bit about your past."

"In my lifetime, there have been many men who I wouldn't have walked across the street to see. Let alone stay with. Did you get my message?"

Five-bye, loud and clear I said. I have the utmost respect and admiration for you. Plus a few other things thrown in. I might add, that I have never know a woman so up-front, honest and caring. She is by far the best catch on Puget Sound.

I brought up the possibility of leaving for Moscow tomorrow, I would have to pack and load some of the car tonight, I asked her what she thought. "Can I go catch a fish first?" That is what I was thinking.

This is not an old-fisherman's tale; but Asia did catch a nine-pound (somewhat-small) but pretty silver-salmon. "Okay, let's get something to eat and then go pack for our trip to Idaho." "I didn't know fishing was so easy." I didn't comment.

When we got back to the apartment, Asia mentioned she wanted to show me the pocketbook she purchased at the airport in New York. The book was written by David Lasswell and was titled: AT HIGH TIDE. I said that was a crazy title. "I don't think so." She stated. "The book has several nautical stories of his friends and family."

"The story I liked best was about a junior high and high school friend of about forty-five years who Lasswell was quite close to." "The friend's name is Faith Wright, respected oil-painting artist who lives in Gig Harbor. "

"Mentioned is the fact they have been at the same reunion several times, have had many meals together but have never had a real date between them." "Faith reported that they held hands once. David wrote it was to help her get across the street."

"I think there are better writers than Lasswell, but he is the best storyteller, that I have ever read." "Silas, you would like the book.

When I was on active duty in the Marine Corps, I volunteered and coached some youth sports. I read and got some important pointers from his book: COACH – WHAT'S UP. It was very enjoyable.

Later, I took Asia to one of our 'boarding houses' for dinner. She soon understood the phrase: 'boarding-house-reach'. She loved the peach pie for dessert.

On the way to the apartment, I stopped for a tank of gas. Asia, also got an evening cup of Folgers coffee for her.

I had left a lot of clothes at my dad's before coming to Seabeck. I still had two-big-bags, plus a little bag plus my cosmetic bag as well.

We both set out our clothes we were going to wear tomorrow and all but one of the bags were put into the car. I said, be sure to keep out a jacket for when you need it.

We wanted to catch the seven-forty ferry out of Bremerton and left in time to stop at Swedes for a bagel and coffee. When we got to Bremerton, it had started to sprinkle a little. I told Asia that this amount of rain in the Pacific Northwest was known as playable mist. "Why?" I didn't answer that either.

We barely made the ferry because of so many cars and people, but arriving in Seattle, we rolled slowly off the ferry, up to Alaska Way and finally to Interstate Five, through the tunnel onto Interstate 90 and across the Lake Washington Floating Bridge. "Is this bridge actually floating?"

I looked at my cheap but accurate Timex and the dials showed nine-thirty-five. How about lunch at Websters in Ellensburg less than four hours from now? "Ellensburg," she asked. Yes, Central Washington University is there plus a lot of good places to eat. "Sounds good to me."

After a couple of minutes of silence, Asia began talking again. "I want to tell you about my daughter." "Are you ready for this?" Absolutely.

"My girl, who I love dearly, had a birth defect when born and it created a hearing loss function in which she has suffered with for years." "Besides having a hearing loss issue, she doesn't like to listen, even when she can hear you."

"She took the loss of her father very hard and has decided that it was everyone's fault but the aircraft; the real cause." "She is staying now in Colorado with my late husband's side of the family."

"She likes seeing me but tires of my visits very quickly. His grandmother is raising her and they get along splendidly." "She is the type who loves gifts but not visitors."

Where does that place you? "At first, I was not good with it, but now, I can understand it better. She was always daddy's little girl. In time I think she will grow out of it."

"Her dad always told her she was special; I think she was unfortunate. She is a bright child and has great reasoning skills. Yes, she is very spoiled." "That the shortened version of the story of my daughter. "

I think my little sister, who was kidnapped, was spoiled too. My folks were both very gracious with both of us and each of us was given things we really didn't need. I can certainly see that possibility while living with a loving grandmother.

"Her grandmother is a former teacher and my daughter is being homeschooled and made to work. That part of the story, I truly like and appreciate. My late husband's mother comes from the old school. There is a time to play and a time to work."

I see nothing in this shortened version of the story which would have me change anything in our relationship. You are my guidance, direction, and magnificent friend. So much appreciated.

Our lunch at Webster's was great. Their hamburgers with cheese, sauces and all of the goodies were terrific. I didn't call it a cheeseburger because the cheese was next to the lettuce. Fries were fine, the rest stop was used to the fullest and back on the road.

As Willie Nelson sang about years ago: "On the road again as we go down the highway." Next wide spot on the road: the Tri-Cities.

When we were having lunch in Ellensburg, the clouds were getting really dark with a threat of heavy rain. Well, about nineteen miles out of Pasco we had winds, heavy rains and the visibility was basically gone.

The window wipers couldn't carry off the down-pour from the windshield. About one-mile down the highway, we luckily saw a rest area. We pulled in and found a safe place to park when tree branches and other things couldn't be blown against the car or fall on it. It was there that we sat.

With the rains continuing the downpour, we decided that if we could get to Pasco, we would stop for the night, I would call my dad and say we will be in tomorrow morning. Asia was all in favor of that.

About an hour later, the rains let up a little, and we drove the highway where portions of it had standing water on it. It was slow going but eventually, we saw the highway sign WA-26 and we turned on to it. I told Asia we are now about one-hundred-twenty-five miles to dads in Moscow.

On the right side of the road, there was a Shiloh Inn. Asia asked, "Do you know this place." Yes, I have stayed in many Shiloh Inns in the Northwest for years.

I pulled the car into their covered entrance area to the building and I went in to register. "Hello Sir, how can I help?" I need two rooms adjoining, my boss and I are traveling together. "I have two, just alike on the third floor."

"Are either of your current military or prior military?" We both are former military. I was a Marine and she is retired Air Force.

I filled out the registration cards for both of us, paid with a credit card and picked up the two door entrance cards and headed back to the car. "How did it go?" Well, I said. We each have a room adjoining on the third floor just off of the elevator.

Why don't you go into the building and I'll get our bag? I will park close by and be there within moments. There was no sun in Pasco, only dark clouds and heavy rain and yes, I got wet. I kept Asia dry and warm.

We opened the doors to both rooms. Inside was another door to open inward when a large family needed two rooms. We opened both doors.

I grabbed a towel out of the bathroom, dried off, found my clean pants in the suitcase and got out of my wet shoes. I felt much better. If it stops raining, later we can go and eat dinner; there is a Denney's Restaurant next door.

Being on the third floor, you could hear every thunderclap, wind howling and the rain pounding the windows. Asia spoke first. "I guess you could say that this wasn't a walk in the park."

I picked up the phone, got an outside dial-tone and dialed my dad's phone number. He answered with the question. "Where are you?" A little outside of Pasco. We hit a major storm and will be there before noon tomorrow if the Lord is willing. "Good." He spoke.

"I am glad that you called, I have a major question for you to answer." "I want you to meet a very good female friend when you are here. Are you willing?" Why certainly, I replied. "Good, she will be here tomorrow when you get here."

The weather had cleared by morning, we had the easy-free breakfast at the Inn and headed down the highway toward Moscow. When we drove past the Washington State University cut-off in Pullman, I told Asia we have about ten miles to go. It went by quickly.

This is the house that dad purchased when we came here from Bremerton. This place has been renovated several times and was once owned by another University of Idaho professor with the last name of Spiker.

My dad and his friend greeted Asia Lynn like she was the queen that she is. Hugs, naturally. The two of us were introduced to a very attractive fifty-five-year-old woman, a Professor of Literature at the U of I.

She wasn't very tall, didn't weigh very much and had a beautiful smile. Her name was Brenda

Ann Hope. She said with a smile. "Ever since I was a kid, I always had hope with me." I thought she was lovely.

After lunch, the four of us sat down in the comfortable-living-room. My dad asked the first question. "How is the relationship going with you two?" Asia jumped in with an answer. "We haven't known each other very long, however, both of us enjoy each other's company. Your son is a complete, genuine gentleman."

"I have a thirteen-year-old daughter who is still reeling from losing her father three years ago. Out of respect for my late-husband and the thoughts of my daughter; I felt it was duty to wait five or six years to even consider another marriage."

"Silas and I are very close working related partners who will travel together, work professionally together and as times goes on will find the correct and fitting conclusion together." "I am honored by his close association." "I am appreciated, respected, probably admired, and catered too. And all that is special."

Then Asia surprised me. "What about the two of you?"

My dad took the question as a perfect opportunity. "It has been a dozen years since the death of Silas's mother. Brenda and I have known each other for about eight years. Her late husband died in a car crash on I-84 years ago. We have dated on and off for several years and we too enjoy each other's company."

My dad excused himself for a couple of minutes, returned and asked Brenda to stand. I watched my dad get down on one knee and asked Brenda to be his wife. She cried and said yes and dad put an engagement ring on her left hand.

Asia and I both jumped up and hugged both of them. In our eyes, the event was beautiful. My dad wanted to ask Brenda to marry him in front of both of us. Asia's blue eyes were dancing and tears were coming down her cheeks. What a wonderful event and day.

When things got back to normal again, it was decided that we would have dinner at an Italian Restaurant in Moscow that evening and tomorrow by six o'clock in the morning dad would drive us to the International Airport in Spokane to fly to Chicago and on to Tampa.

Later that day, I made arrangements in St. Pete to be picked up in the late-afternoon the following day in Florida. I told Providers that I would meet up with Asia Lynn and we would be at the airport in Tampa together by pick-up time.

After my call about ten minutes later; Blake Tate called and said we could have a couple more days if we wanted it because Alan had been involved in a car wreck in San Antonio and

Savannah had flown to San Antonne to be with him.

I answered without asking my boss for her opinion. I told Blake to let's go with the original schedule. "So be it." He replied. "Enjoy the visit with your dad."

I told the other three what Blake had told me and it was Asia who said, "Let me say a prayer out loud for Alan." She did.

The drive to the airport to Spokane was easy, once we got the car loaded. Asia hugged my dad and told him to thank you. I hugged him and shook his hand and quietly asked him: what do you think? "I think she is perfect for you if that was your question." I smiled back at him.

A porter took us and the baggage to the check-in at United and we booked to Chicago and on to Tampa. Arrival time in Florida was four-forty-two. We both got to St. Pete at eight-ten and were taken to our new suites the company-owned. We moved in next door to each other.

CHAPTER ELEVEN:
TROUBLE IN TEXAS

It seemed like we were relaxed and eager to hear from Mr. Tate the up-date on Alan and Savannah. Mr. Tate asked, "Do any of either of you want to talk about items from your break?"

I said it was great weather in the Northwest and it was great seeing my dad. I was the only comment.

"That's fine." "Then let's begin. I will start with a couple of announcements and I will also begin our session on diplomacy. We are going to cut that down to a couple of days."

I have a big announcement to make about your foreign-language up-date. The Nightclouds, Horatio and his wife will be your instructor on the Country of Spain Spanish language. "Wow." Asia said. Surprise, I replied.

"This will be brand new to you. The company is going to send the two of you to Spain by yourselves." "There are several reasons."

"When you were gone, a primarily all African American Church here in Saint Pete called and then followed with a letter asking us for assistance in acquiring information if we could do a formal analysis of the current situation where once the genocide occurred in Rwanda in 1994."

"We have for a few years wanted to do that. The Rwandan Government has allowed our company the right to visit and identify what could be done in the region where between 1990 and 1994 during their civil war a total of nearly one-half a million were killed in the genocide." "There were twenty-thousand murdered in the area of the Nyanubaye Catholic Church. That's about sixty miles East of Kigali, Rwanda."

"We have asked Alan and Savannah if they would make that trip and project their first when Alan is ready to travel in the near future." "We were pleased when they replied: yes."

"One other thing. If the two of you continue to work well together as a pair in reaching out to foreign countries; that is what we will do in Europe, the Med and in the Far East." "Would the two of you like that?" There were smiles from both of us.

Let me give my opening concept and thought process on diplomacy."

"Normally, Corporate Executive work on improving diplomacy on three levels, Internal, External and Public Approval. They must prevent a fair and honest presentation to their employees and executive staff."

"The diplomacy with other corporations is necessary to allow for growth and expansion. Through media presentation and public relations releases, the public must see and witness the effort first hand."

"Diplomacy is a mainline management function. Built and maintained by executive officers. These people can't pass the buck to others without giving quality training and understanding on where the corporation stands on issues."

"Our officers and spokespeople must bring others into the fold without offending, disturbing the status quo, by not overstepping their position and allowing for others to be trained, well-educated on the topic and able to explain the position in full detail."

"In a way, to keep our diplomacy in an honorable position; we must maintain friendships with others, keeping others away who are trying to hurt us; and make them unable to perform those functions without suffering the consequences."

"We separate the wheat from the shaft every day. Those we respect and those who respect us, must never lose the diplomacy extended. Others we want to include in the future must have every chance of learning and living the philosophy we are presenting."

"The points I have highlighted is where you will come in representing us with foreign-country governments."

"Why don't the two of you go get familiar with the facilities and we will start tomorrow with the Nightclouds after their arrival." We were excused.

I looked at Asia and asked her a question. Is there more to this than what Blake Tate is letting us in on?

"I thought that myself," "Only time will tell us and today and this evening we will have time to work on the list of phrases, sayings, words, etc. that Horatio had faxed to us. "Oh, I had forgotten about those." She said with a smile.

I added to her remark. Even by learning some of these we will not know the emphasis, real verbal punctuation of these without having the help of the two of them. "Agreed."

When we got to the apartments, we opened the inside doors so the apartments would be considered one apartment.

We decided that she would call Alaska and Texas and I would call Wyoming and Idaho.

I dialed my dad's number in Moscow and he answered, "Good morning, how are you?" We are both fine and wanted to know how you two were. "I do have some news. When I got back taking the two of you to Spokane; Brenda and I went by the court house and got our marriage license." I asked when the wedding is?

"It already happened. We were married by a Judge we know at the Court House and were married in his chambers. Two professors from the University stood up for us as witnesses."

That's outstanding. I think I will be calling your wife either mom or Brenda "I know that she will like that."

When I got through to Jasper, I gave him the up-date on Alan and told him that my dad just got married. I told him as far as I know, Asia and I are still planning to come to Wyoming for his. I told him I would keep him posted and somewhat up to date.

I asked him where his assignment was. He said this will be hard to swallow; but we are going to Fort Carson, just South of Colorado Springs. Boy are you lucky.

Asia told me that she talked to Katarina's mother in Valdez who said Kat was overseas chasing bad guys. It is something she always wanted to do. Kat's mother also told Asia how sorry she was for the loss of her husband. "We have always supported the military here in Alaska at Anchorage, Fairbanks and on Adak. And naturally all-over the world."

When Asia heard Kat's mother speaking about her husband; she realized that Katarina must have told her mother too about Savannah, Alan and Jasper. So, Asia brought Kat's mother up to date.

When Asia called Savannah in San Antonio, she received some news that was worse than what we first heard. Alan had some internal injuries than we first heard with broken ribs and other complications. Savannah told Asia, that it could be two to three weeks before Alan could get out of the hospital.

The driver of the car that Alan was in is doing better now. A lot of bumps and bruises, but not broken bones. He is younger than Alan. Savannah said, she was sorry to report that the old man driving the other car, had a severe heart attack while driving and he has since passed away.

Savannah also said that the wife of the older man who passed; has come to the hospital to visit both Alan and the younger driver. She was in tears for all concerned.

When those topics were gone from under the bridge and down the river; Savannah told Asia that she and Alan are not sure if they will stay with Providers. I feel that I need to stay and help Alan recover and Alan is not sure if he is going to be able to take international travel and the rigors of the job.

When all of the calls were made, Asia Lynn and I discussed each call-in detail. Asia told me, "I think that I have to call and tell Mr. Tate what Savannah just told her."

Asia, got a hold of Mr. Tate by phone and gave the up-date. He asked, "Could the two of us come back this afternoon for further discussion on the situation?" The answer was that we would leave in just a few minutes.

Mr. Tate was in nice suit and Asia and I were dressed very casually. The conversation was very relaxed and very open. He asked, "if we had any ideas?" I said yes. This is only a concept I said.

Please don't change you concept about Rwanda. There is one person that could go as the primary contact and do an outstanding job. He said, "Who is that?" I told him Della Faye Sharp. Anybody could travel with her. She is so well-spoken, comes across so cleanly, and has the mind and the brains to do a perfect job.

I finished my thought with the following. If Alan and Savannah do come back in time; they could pick up at that time. However, if they don't come back, Providers is still on schedule and head of the game. We can't let the Church down in St. Pete. Asia jumped in and spoke. "Why can't the Church provide a male person to assist Della on the trip?"

With a smile on his face, Mr. Tate noted, "I don't know if we pay you two enough monies." Instantly, also with a smile on her face, Asia spoke, "probably not."

We were asked to wait and within five-minutes Blake Tate was back with Mr. Williamson. "Hello you two," he said.

Mr. Tate retold Mr. Williamson about the concept. Mr. Williamson listened and was well tuned into the thought. He sat in his chair for a moment, looked at the ceiling and finally spoke, "why not?" Then the big boss left and Mr. Tate invited Della Faye Sharp to join us.

When Della saw the two of us, we each received a very warm hug. When Della entered the room, she was still walking with a swagger that identified her importance and her position in life. He body's manner publicly said there is nothing that she could not do. When she sat down, then came the repeat of the story you just heard.

"I am flattered." "I had no idea you would consider me beyond my normal duties." "I would love the opportunity she said. Do I get to pick my partner from that Church?" Asia said. "It could be Mr. Right." Even Mr. Tate laughed.

Asia Lynn and myself went back to the apartments at peace with ourselves. She said, "let's go play putt-putt, I think I can beat you." We did, she did.

In a short time after returning to the apartments, my phone rang and it was Horatio and asked, "where are you guys?" Let's begin by asking where you are?

"Mr. Tate said we would be staying in the location for a week as to where Alan was going to be staying." Well, you are two doors down from where we are. Open your front door and come down to see us.

Both of us went outside in front of our apartments and sure enough, walking down the street toward us was Horatio and his wife Priscilla. More hugs and more introductions.

Priscilla Nightcloud was nearly Asia's height, was slender in builder, wore brightly colored clothes and presented a wonderful and beautiful smile with glorious white teeth and beautiful black, well-manicured hair.

Horatio smiled and acted like he just concurred the world by being in Florida again and so soon. "What's up with you two?"

I started to talk but Asia jumped in with, "we are living the dream and have been very busy with work and some pleasure." We invited them in to my apartment, offered a beverage, they accepted; and I primarily told them all that we had learned with phone calls earlier in the day. I am really looking forward to it."

On the coffee table in Silas' room was Lasswell's book. "I brought it over for Silas to read it." Horatio said. "I have read and enjoyed his two novels: CORPSMEN CHRONICLES and CORPSMEN CHRONICLES II. "I think Lasswell is a wordsmith." Asia offered. "I think he is the best storyteller that I have ever read."

Horatio then said something that surprised me. "I still don't know why a language needs to be taught to the two of you because everywhere you will be going to, non-speaking English governments will have quality interpreters."

"My concept." He spoke is, "you should be learning just enough to have the host nation think you have been schooled before getting there. They want you there and they want and need the company's talents to help them overcome." I agreed completely.

"If the company is going to send you to countries in the Med and in Europe, are they actually going to take the time, money and other expenses for you to learn Greek, Turkish, Italian, and other languages of the Azores, Crete, Sicily, and even Iran?" "I doubt it."

"We are happy to be here, but I think you two and Della don't have to go through all of this." We both agreed with him.

"How are your kids and where are they staying?"

"They are staying the week with some friends in the highlands of New Mexico."

"All four of them are happy we are in Florida and this beautiful weather."

"I want to give the two of you a fair and honest break with language, but I am going to be honest with Mr. Tate and others here that with assistance from others where you are visiting, we and others can't teach you enough in a one week's time."

"We are good, but not that good."

Asia asked. "Where are you planning to have dinner this evening?" "Here, with you guys in this beautiful complex. How is the food?" It is absolutely delicious, I said.

The two of us took the Native American and his Spanish woman for a walk and tour of the complex and showed most of the sights and games to be played along the way.

Horatio's phone rang and it was Mr. Tate wanted to know if they were here yet. "Yes, we are here walking the grounds with Asia and Silas." "Would you like to have dinner with the four of us?" "Can we make it six and I can bring my friend with me?"

"Certainly." "What is your friend's name?" "Her name is Della; you might remember her." I told him to tell Mr. Tate that we will see them at six o'clock. Horatio did just that.

It was a dinner or fun and laughs and business wasn't mentioned once. Tomorrow at eight o'clock it will be back to normal again.

We all went back to our lodging and in our apartments, each of us stayed home but the door between us was open.

I thought the presentation Horatio gave Asia and I about the language challenge was outstanding. However, the repeat presentation he gave Mr. Tate that morning was spot on and nearly perfect. Blake Tate had absolutely nothing to fall back on and lacked any opportunity to challenge or question his thinking.

"I think that Mr. Williamson has to hear a repeat of your presentation Horatio, let me see if I can get him." The two of them were back in a flash.

Again, Mr. Williamson was back in the board room hearing a challenge to his ruling on language presentation. "You made a hell of a presentation, Horatio." "So, what are you saying in one statement?"

"Mr. Williamson, the company needs the language presentations, not these two or three that are going directly to the governments. It the people of and in the fields that have to be able to communicate." "Della and these two are off the charts; just let them go to work and perform."

"Blake, would you come with me for a couple of minutes?" Out the door they went.

It took about ten-minutes before Mr. Tate returned. Tate asked the question to Horatio. "How long would you two like to stay in Florida?" The answer was this. "We would like to stay this week since we are here already and give Asia and Silas an overview of Spain's Spanish."

"Consider that done. Now, are you open to a proposal?"

"Sure."

"Would the two of you consider the possibility of moving to Florida and taking a position here as the Director of International Languages?"

The lady originally from Spain was smiling, and the Native American who spoke Osage fluently also smiled and spoke. "Can you give me a minute to think about it? I have thought about it and the answer is yes." There were tears, laughter and hugs.

When I think about this: Horatio and Priscilla are coming to St. Pete. Alan and Savannah are in San Antonio, maybe not coming back. Della, is going to travel to Africa and Rwanda. Jasper and Janet are going just a few minutes South of the Springs in Colorado in the Army. Katarina is chasing bad guys overseas and Asia and I are living a dream waiting for the shoes to hit the floor. Wow!

At that time, a messenger came in with a note for Mr. Tate. He read the note and then began to speak. "The note was from the staff at Kindred Hospital in San Antonio: Doctors have found a hole in Alan's left lung, and there will be surgery later today. Be sure to pray for him."

Mr. Blake Tate, never lost for words added. "Your Spanish language from Spain starts now."

It was Horatio who asked us to bow our heads as he began his prayer for Alan. We all did. The prayer was short but right to the point. "Alan has had it tough; it's time he if left to recover."

Priscilla passed out a clean copy of the two-hundred and fifty words and phrases that were faxed from Horatio previously. She spoke, "I think I am going to just read for you the words and phrases so you can hear them correctly before you start learning each one." After I listened very carefully to her emphasis in each one; I realized this was not going to be a piece-of-cake.

Horatio's next comment made a lot of sense to me. "On your work page, make a check-mark on one through seven, eleven, twelve and thirteen. These are going to be the primary greetings and good-bye messages that you will learn."

Horatio began to read these ten off; over and over again. "Have you listened to the strength and emphasis on each phrase?" "This time I will listen to Silas say each one; slowly and one-at-a-time." "Not bad for a beginner."

Asia was next to recite the phrases. She sounded as if she was from Barcelona. The first time I heard her pronunciation, I knew who would be tutoring whom. By the time that the class session was over late afternoon, we had gone through fifty-words and phrases and had said them perhaps fifty-times each.

It might be crazy to say this, but I do know the meaning and have learned to understand some of them quite well. Two hundred more to go and four more days to do them in with quality instruction.

Horatio and Priscilla are dear friends but, importantly are very sincere in trying to prepare us for off-the-cuff comments when we visit Madrid. Today was a very good session.

Blake Tate stuck his head through the door and spoke. "It is time to call it a day. See the four of you in the morning."

The days passed quickly, but the lessons were not easy. Priscilla, was as tough as nails in getting the sound of each as close to perfect as possible. Her statement which summed it all up was spot-on. "I am complimenting both of you on your work and efforts; you did very well. I have been saying most of these for over fifty-years. You two five days."

We said our goodbyes to Horatio and Priscilla and they were off to pack and on to the airport for their flight back to New Mexico. We would see them again soon, in about ten days and they would have their children with them.

The two of us walked to have dinner before heading back to the apartments. Asia asked, "How do you think we did?" Don't ask me. I am only an Associate Director.

I went on to add. Both of them said you were near perfect in your Spain Spanish language-sound emphases and pronunciation. Honestly, you dazzled me.

I checked my phone for messages when we got to the apartment and there was one from Jasper. "The marriage will not be held on October 15. The Army had me move up my sign-in date. Yes, we are now married; but it was a Justice-Of-the-Peace in Cheyenne who performed the ceremony. Our parents were there with us."

I am very happy that Jasper and Janet have started their life together. Both of us were looking forward to meeting her and both families at the wedding and also having another road-trip together even it was flying. That must wait now until we head to Spain.

My phone rang shortly after we had dinner. I answered it, and the voice on the other end of the line said his name was Jason Robert O'Dea. I am with the African American Christian Church here in town and I was told by a representative of Providers that I should contact you and come meet with you and Asia before seeing the players involved on Monday about Rwanda.

"Is it possible to meet with you and Asia tomorrow, Saturday. You decide the time?" Jason, let me check with Asia for a moment and I will be right back-on-the-line. Asia had over-heard portions of the conversation and was smiling. "Sure, why not?"

Yes, I told him we would love to do that and would ten in the morning be alright with you? We could meet at my apartment and the three of us could have a very private conversation. I gave Jason my address and I told him to come very casual.

"What a very gracious sounding individual." Asia remarked. "Who do you think told him about us?" I couldn't hold back. I think it was Della Faye Sharp, herself. She trusts us, approves of us, is comfortable with us and knows that if we support Jason's position, Della would be very appreciative.

Our breakfast in the morning was over at nine-twenty and we went right-directly to the apartment. At ten, the doorbell rang. I opened the door and standing there was a handsome black man in casual clothes with a big smile. "Hello," he said. "I'm Jason."

Jason O'Dea, was about six-feet tall, perhaps one-hundred-eighty-pounds, like Jasper was all muscle and still military fit. He told us that he has been out of the Army now about ninety days.

"An opportunity doesn't come along every day for a chance to benefit my new Church and the people of Rwanda." "What can you tell me about Della Sharp?" Asia answered with "she is one of the most talented women I have met in my entire life." "She could do anything in the world she wanted to and I think she is gifted."

"How about the top brass at Providers?" If you just be yourself, I said. You will do well. "Providers is loaded with some well-qualified management group and sharp employees," Asia spoke.

Asia's phone rang and she ran through the connecting doors to answer it. "Yes, he is here; certainly, come on over." "We will see you in about ten minutes." Asia looked like she swallowed a canary when she came back. "Della will be here in about ten minutes."

Jason told us that he has only spoken with Della for about three minutes on the phone. He is looking forward to meeting her. Again, Asia remarked. "Jason, Della is as beautiful as you are handsome. You will make a good-looking couple in your life and travels."

The door-bell rang and Asia went to answer the door. "Come in." When they saw each other, I think they were both impressed with the other's appearance. There might have been sparks, but I didn't see any.

Della, I said, we are just getting to know Jason and now it is your turn to catch up. "I would like that." Della, also added. "I couldn't think of any two betters to break-the-ice with Jason; then you two."

I recapped the conversation so far. Jason, retired from the Army three months ago and has been accepted to begin an appointment to a Seminary when school starts the next semester. You should be back from Rwanda by then. He is thirty-eight years old and a very strong Christian.

Asia and I think he would be perfect to protect you and assist you in various ways overseas in Africa. He has our endorsement. Can we treat the two of you to lunch? "Good heavens, yes." Della said.

During lunch, the three of us, outlined the game plan and concept that Providers had for Della's trip and possible future. Maybe, I said to Jason; you might have to change you schedule pertaining to the seminary. I told Jason that I have seen the ball bounce in many different directions. You never know where it is going.

I paid the bill, left the tip and Asia and I headed home to the apartments. Della and Jason were still there.

Asia said. "Monday morning is going to be very interesting." "I would like to be able to hear the interview." Good idea, I said. Maybe we can all here the interview and add comments.

On Monday morning, before class time, I called Mr. Tate and asked if we could participate and he said, "I will ask referencing that the three of you would be helping him with the introduction to the company." That's fair I thought.

When it was time to start the day at eight; Mr. Tate gave me a thumb-up. Tate said, "if it is alright with Jason O'Dea, it is alright with Providers. When the time comes, he would ask the first two or three questions."

The other two didn't let the cat out of the bag about the day before, including lunch and when Jason came into the room he shook hands with Della, Asia, myself and then Mr. Tate.

Blake Tate began with the welcome, looking forward to the interview; thanking Jason for volunteering and stepping forward on behalf of his Church. Jason smiled and spoke, "Thank you, I am delighted to be here."

Jason knew he was amongst friends and acted that way; very relaxed and extremely well-polished. Mr. Tate started with where were you from and basic, general information.

"I was born and raised in Moses Lake, Washington. I come from a very strong Christian background. My father was a lay minister and my mother the organ player at Church.

"I was an outstanding student and athlete in high school and had three-scholarship offers to play small-college football at Whitworth, Idaho State and Boise State. Back then Boise State was not like it is today; knocking off the big-boys."

When in high school my junior and senior years I worked part-time at a radio-station in Moses Lake: KSEM-Radio. I did sport newscast late afternoons and on the weekends.

"My dad was a member of the Marine Corps and he and my mother talked about all of the benefits of a military service career. I certainly now understand the retirement benefits of a pension, medical care and appreciation shown by society for those who have served."

Mr. Tate added, "Asia is an Air Force retired Lieutenant Colonel and Silas served in the Marine Corps for six years." Jason thanked the two of us for serving.

Jason continued. "My unit was one of the first of the Army who went into Baghdad. There were other fun stops as well." "I didn't get to Baghdad, I was in training at Fort Benning and on my thirteenth jump, I landed strangely and broke my ankle in two places. No more jumping for me. The Army wanted to know if I wanted to stay in and find another career field. Yes, I did."

"They asked me what else I had done? And I mentioned the radio work in high school. I was assigned to Fort Ben Harrison in Indiana in AFRTS broadcast training. I went there as a student and was also assigned there twice as an instructor. When not with AFN or AFRTS overseas, I was a public affairs specialist and technician for nine of my twenty years." "I loved all of it." "When it really gets cold, my foot still tells me about that jump at Benning."

"I will be thirty-nine when my birthday gets here in a couple of weeks."

When it was my time to ask my first question. "Are you familiar with the location of Rwanda and the location where the genocides occurred seven-to-ten years ago?"

"Yes, I have been well informed and by my reading of the events and why and how they happened." "A complete and absolute shame and the loss of one-half-million lives are horrible even to think about."

Asia asked. "Could and would you keep our Della safe and protected?" "Asia, I have been trained to do just that. Take my word for it; I would give up my life long before we could lose hers." "It would be part of my duties to keep us both safe."

Della asked the questions that hit the nail on the head. "Explain to us why you would want to go? Is it who you are?" "I would love to go to help start the process of eliminating poverty in the country. I have witnessed poverty first hand in the country after country. When my pastor at Church asked if I would consider the opportunity; my luggage was ready to be packed."

For the second question Jason answered. "Yes, it is me to the tee. I don't see skin color, issues with male or female; I see people, conditions, opportunity, a chance for improving, caring, giving and helping in solving problems."

"I have been blessed even going through this interview." "Mr. Tate, I am a straight shooter and I publicly want to tell you that I spent time on Saturday with the three of them. It included a question-and-answer session and also lunch."

Mr. Blake Tate spoke, "Jason, I am glad you said that. I already knew that because Silas told me when he called this morning."

"If the four of you will excuse me for about ten minutes; I want to go tell Mr. Williamson, that we have found our man."

When the boss closed the door, Asia said. "Welcome aboard." Jason said, "Thank you, but I want to hear it from the Director of Human Resources."

It was even better than that, Tate brought Mr. Williamson back with him who said, "It is nice to meet you and Providers would like to offer you a position.

It took Jason about three hours to go through HR, salary discussions, position title, insurance, passport, and other goodies.

Later, after lunch, Mr. Tate joined the four of us to review company policy, diplomacy, international travel, logistics, responsibilities and procedures. Jason brought us back to our senses quickly with the comment. "This is the first trip overseas with this company for all of us." He was right.

Jason is taking the apartment on the other side of Della. When you look on our street at the apartments from left to right is mine, Asia, Della and soon-to-be Jason's. When Horatio and family get here their double suite, which includes space for their children, will be around the corner and the second apartment from Jason's end unit. They have a total of five-bedrooms and three-bathrooms.

The larger the new family grows in number, the greater the value of the company rises. From the former military point of view; we have Air Force, Army, Navy and Marine Corps members. We are also sisters and brothers with different mothers in Christ.

Jason, with Della's leadership, compassion, and mutual understanding, is off to a very excellent start. They will be in our prayers.

I asked Asia if she had said anything to any of her friends about me? "Maybe one or two only. Why?" Well, I got a nice letter from your friend Grace, who gave me some great insight on you.

Grace said she got to know you in the military and that she worked for you once and you have been friends ever since. This is what she said about you: You were an excellent cook but you would rather make reservations than a recipe. You hated to do all of the dishes. But you have had a beautiful house. You don't believe in doing laundry, you like to send some it out to be done.

She said you had a beautiful inner soul. You are a person of great character, a very strong Christian, and last but not least, a fantastic artist and fashion designer. Did she give you a fair assessment? "Quite close to the truth."

Asia said, "let me tell you about Grace." "The most kind and gracious person I ever met. She is probably more lovely than I am on the inside and out. She too is a pen-and-ink artist and wants to do fashion design sometime during her life. She is the best friend a person could find." "We look and act an awful much alike." "She has a heart of gold." "All peoples love her."

"She has a heart to care for people she doesn't even know. She is the world's first-class Christian and "natural prayer. She knows exactly what to say and do." "She occasionally cries just to shed some tears to make more room in her heart."

"She is very easy to love." "She is more like a sister than anyone else I know." "On a scale of one to ten; she is more like a twelve."

You are so elaborate with her information; I wonder what you might have said about me. "Why don't you ask Grace?". Why do you think she sent me the note without her return address? "She knew that I wouldn't answer your question and she didn't think she had too either."

CHAPTER TWELVE:
SAD STORIES COMING OUT

I have recently seen some great pairings of people at Providers. We heard a very unsettling story told by Blake Tate, the loss of his wife. A horrible story about Alan Carpenter, and the car wreck and an equally up-setting story of Savannah Whitlock, with her parent's divorce proceedings.

But more truth, than fiction; we have seen Horatio and Priscilla, being returned to St. Pete. Jasper and Janet, being married in Cheyenne. Savannah, being by Alan's side in San Antonio. Also, Della and Jason being paired with great futures and opportunities. And yes, I can't leave out my very talented boss.

I asked Asia Lynn if she would come and listen to an idea that I wanted to bring to the attention of Blake Tate and the higher-ups. She said she would and came over with a cup of coffee. "Hot and strong." She spoke. I didn't comment, but I agreed with her.

Asia, I have been doing some private research, not with company guidance, but only on my own about the expected amount of wasted cash the company spends on not having an office in

Europe. Long flights and expenses are killing the company.

I have studied maps of the main portion of Europe and realize from Wiesbaden, Germany by car, you can literally go almost everywhere. Four-hours from Amsterdam. Less than five to Paris and the list goes on.

It we are going to concentrate on attacking European cities with high unemployment and a staggering poverty level; why not put our group of presenters, language experts, and a few-teams of trade leaders in Europe than continue to fly them again and again across the pond.

You can't put the company on the coast-line in Europe but in the center where it is close to cities in any direction. Within five-hours of Wiesbaden you can drive from Wiesbaden to Amsterdam, and Wiesbaden to Paris. From Wiesbaden to Frankfort, it takes about forty-minutes. Many communities are located in between those times and distances.

I wouldn't go so far as to say move the entire operations; but in the next three-years we are in Europe and the Med; make it simple on all involved. We the people in the company could and should have working vias' not only passports.

I don't believe that it doesn't have to be Wiesbaden but Wiesbaden was the least expensive, closest to most locations than other communities in the general area.

I would love to live in Europe, work there and be able to travel nearly anywhere wanted with a couple of days free. Don't you think that cities looking for our assistance would relish the thought that we were just down the street instead of being over the Atlantic?

Before you answer let me finish with this thought. We basically could make two presentations a week if we were just a few short hours away from the destination. Asia, what do you think?

"Silas, I think you are a genius and I can't wait for you to approach the company with the idea." "I would love to be in Europe with you. You know, I love to travel and do road trips."

"About your comments about the pairing of couples did you leave us out for a reason?" I don't believe we are in a major hurry based on our discussion of your late husband, and your teenage daughter. You know that I care deeply. Let's just see what three-years will bring. I don't think that either one of us wants to lose the other. "Very true." She agreed.

"Reference Mr. Tate, why not bring it up tomorrow before Horatio and Priscilla get back and we attack Spain's Spanish again." "We might be expanding our time in Europe after this trip to Spain." "I would like that."

I always think that Blake Tate asks the question. "What is coming next from this group?" I don't think it hurts any to try to improve the situation for the company. Asia, should I call him first this morning or just bring it up? "I think he likes surprises." "Just bring it up." So, I did.

He gave me an opportunity to do 'my opinion' publicly. Mr. Tate was one and three others: Asia, Della, and Jason. "This is different than what we looked at before. I will pass it along later this afternoon." "I will have them run numbers."

About four o'clock Mr. Williamson came into the room, quietly pulled up a chair, sat down and waited for him to be recognized by Blake. "What gives us the honor sir?"

"I came to tell Silas what I have done. I gave the proposal or thought to three of our best 'money' minds in the company. I did not want them to work together but for each of them to draw their own conclusion and report back." "They have."

"Silas, I was stunned by their findings. They all, individually, came up with answers that agree with you across the board." "Why Wiesbaden?"

I looked at Wiesbaden because the American Air Base is no longer there. Wiesbaden is one of the cheapest costs of living city in the entire country. There is a quality workforce to call on and the poverty-level is far from the highest in the country.

The Amelia Earhart Hotel is averaging fifty-seven-percent nightly rented rooms and office space and living quarters could be arranged very cheaply in the beginning until other arrangement could be made or built. The American Arms Hotel has space as well.

Residence in the community would gladly like to see the influence of an American presence. When you look at Frankfort, Berlin, Ramstein and other locations you are looking at 'big bucks' to operate. The company would enjoy the 'costs of living index' there besides. It's a lovely city.

"How would you go about it from here?" I would have my conversation with Spain and the American Military Commands; however, outside of that, if we could afford it, I would not do anything else in Europe or the Med until we operated out of Wiesbaden or some other place in Europe.

"What would your corporate structure be in Europe?" I would keep two offices, one here; one there. I would have you and your wife living in Wiesbaden. You with the title of owner and President, I would have someone from Germany as your general operating officer.

I would have three-teams of two-people each as points of contact to the other countries and cities. Asia and I would be one-team, Della and Jason another team; and the third team to be named later.

Besides that, I would place satellite offices in perhaps four-countries that could handle local, unexpected issues. I would place Horatio and Priscilla in Barcelona, Spain. Priscilla, knows Barcelona like the back of her hand.

I don't have the names for the teams, but I would eventually put a team in Belgium, Poland, and Norway. There are major cities in all of these great counties. The average person there would not know what our company does, because there are cities in these countries with very-low poverty levels. Our needed personnel and products could come from those locations.

I would have Mr. Carlson run the American office in St. Pete and my manning requirements would be hired from applicants in the United States. I believe we can have local trade-individuals to do initial training, but the parties that reach out to countries should be Americans hired in Florida from throughout the States.

Two of the people I would take in a New York second, if healthy would-be Alan and Savannah. One other area, I would cover ourselves with our own security. We need to protect what is ours. Do you think we could get Katarina to leave the FBI? I do and let her bring some friends with her.

"Would you and Asia like to make this presentation to our Board of Directors?" Certainly, now that you have mentioned that. I think you will need to have an International Board as well or have some of the American representatives' move to Europe to oversee operations. Able to give immediate support.

Lastly, save where the opportunity exists. My opinion is what you asked for. Spinning wheels, cost us thousands of dollars annually.

It took nearly two-weeks for the answer to come down. "Yes, there will be an office and working headquarters in Europe." Then it took another week before we found out that it would be in Wiesbaden.

Asia and I will not take part in this segment of the plan. The experts will have to do that. We have ten-days before we head to Madrid. Including time for a refresher course in Spain's Spanish. Some rewrite of our presentations and plans for when and where we will meet with the American Military Commands.

Asia and I are still spending much time together; but doing individual work and requirements necessary before our travel begins. Priscilla, has worked with me making me better equipped with proper phrases and special words in Spanish.

I don't know how it happens, Asia got her blond-hair cut about three-inches shorter and her blue-eyes sparkle brighter. I come out of a barber-shop and I look like I got ran-over by a dump-truck. It takes about three-days for me to do the re-do.

Asia, the clothes-designer of the future does a fantastic job of selecting appropriate colors for blouses, shirts, slacks and all clothes for each of us including suits and ties. She even suggested that I wear French-Shriners boots on our trip. I plan too.

Tomorrow, we fly. From St. Pete to Orlando in the company's jet and then from Orlando non-stop to Madrid on Lufthansa Airlines. Naturally first class.

Even the air-marshal on the Airliner knows who we are and where we are going. The security is all in place, we each have copies of our speeches and we each are carrying our attaches.

There is no question we are flying on the best of all international carriers. The service is tremendous.

I studied the airline menu and suggested lunch choices to Asia. "Let me see the menu, please." She asked. "I think I will have the teriyaki chicken bowl." It was not what I had suggested.

For the woman who had the tomato soup and grilled-cheese in Seabeck; I thought she might like the chicken-hummus-sandwich. Wrong. I ordered the sandwich for myself.

Traveling with maroon-passports, the ones used by diplomats, places are piece of identity; more important than we actually are. Remember, I am not knocking it. Asia, qualifies, I am not sure it I do or not.

The guy across the aisle asked 'what I did for the government?' I told him, 'I liked spending his money.' He didn't ask another question and quietly went back to his book. Asia said. "He is from a different pay-grade." She then laughed.

We are now both recognized as Provider's International Directors. I work for her because of time and grade. Also, because she is more brilliant, sharper, smarter, and far more beautiful. I also can't leave out talented.

Our pilot, who speaks beautiful English, could be an American. More likely, a well-educated German. Interrupted the quiet with a short announcement of taking the plane off-course for a few-minutes for us not to have to fly into a massive storm over the Atlantic. He said, "We could have rain in Spain for our arrival."

Asia smiles, "the rain in Spain usually falls on the plane." I smiled back and said the word plane is spelled differently. "I don't care, I thought it was funny." It was.

The cabin flight-crew are all multi-lingual, very attractive women; maybe from two or three European countries. They could or might have already posed for the cover of Cosmopolitan.

It took nearly an extra-hour to get to Madrid. We landed safely, no tension-moments at all. The plane's captain was somewhat right. It wasn't really rain, but a down-pour.

Every airport in the world I have been in, I always wanted someone to hold-up my name card for my assistance on my arrival. Asia's name was on the top-line and mine immediately below. We both loved it.

The Hotel sent a driver and a limo to pick us up. There was also another messenger who said the luggage would be brought to our rooms. We were taken to a first-class recognized lodging in the beautiful Pestana Plaza Mayor Madrid Hotel.

The check-in was completed without us signing in and we went directly to the fifth-floor for adjoining matching suites. Once inside, we opened the two-connecting door inside the rooms. Asia said. "This is really up-town." I agreed, but I knew we were down-town and only four-blocks from the Parliament Building.

Like most people, we took care of our clothes and the luggage; the moment the luggage arrived. Are you hungry? I asked. "Not really. Have you looked at the nice baskets we were left?" I will now.

Providers sent us to Madrid one day early for us to get use to the time-change. We were both good the rest of the day and night preparing for the next morning. It was a beautiful day.

The phone in Asia's room rang and the voice saying the government car was ready to pick us up. When in the elevator I told her how lovely and professional she looked. She smiled and said, "Let's go do it."

When it was time to enter the chamber; a Sargant-of-arms type led us into the theater arrangement onto the stage to our seats. We had applause when we entered and when we sat down the parliament members sat down.

We were speaking today to a nice-size crowd. There are three-hundred and fifty deputies and two-hundred and fifty senate members. There were three chairs in from of the other house members. One for the Deputies Director and the other for the President of the Senate. The chair in the middle was for the Prime Minister.

On the stage with us was a small table with the interrupter seated and two flags. One from Spain and the Stars and Stripes of the United States. The spot lights came on over us on stage and also there was a spot light shining on the door we just had entered.

The prime Minister of Spain, Jose M. Aznar was introduced, the Parliament and all stood as one and the march began to play when he entered and advanced to the front of his chair. He smiles at us both.

It was announced that the Anthems of the two countries would be played next. First the Anthem of the Kingdom of Spain. When the Anthem of the United States was played the two of us stood at attention and saluted as we were both still on active-duty. It was amazing.

The interrupter spoke beautiful English and introduced an International Director of Providers Asia Lynn Dash. Then announced the same in Spanish. Director Dash thanked the interrupter, addressed the Prime Minister, the lead chair of the Deputies and the President of the Senate. And finally, to all members of the Parliament.

Asia began her remarks with "the two of us who will speak today will represent Providers International, the government of the United States and perhaps more importantly the peoples of the world who are suffering from poverty."

The eyes and ears of the Prime Minister and the Parliament of Spain were focused on the message presented. There were breaks with applause, a couple of standing responses, and interest and concern shown on the faces. She was getting to their hearts and the heart of the matter.

I have never seen a crowd of this size so quiet during her remarks. When she said this is a universal problem. "Yes, in the United States, Spain and with eighty-seven-percent of the countries of the world."

She reached deep into their souls when she said. "The World can't laugh this one off. We, you and I, must do something about this." "I can't do it by myself, and you can't either."

Asia spoke brilliantly for twenty-five minutes. "You, have heard my message from my heart. Now, within moments you will hear Director Fox's message from his ever-engaging mind." "May God Bless all of us in this endeavor? Thank you."

When she turned toward me, I could see tears falling from her blue eyes. It was one of the best speeches I had heard in my life. Maybe, the only better one given by Doctor Martin Luther King, Jr.

The interrupter used my full-name in the introduction. Listen now to Silas Franklyn Fox. My first thoughts were; here I am in the Court of the Queen, maybe they might think I am a court jester.

I was amazed, the Parliament had been applauding and I had not yet opened my mouth. I thanked the interrupter, addressed the leaders and the Parliament.

I used a Fox-worthy word to make contact instantly. I said, Folks, those were real-tears falling from the eyes of my-partner Asia Lynn Dash. She spoke to you from her heart, I will too in addition to my mind of economics and conditions. I will try not to use American slang or slogans.

If you are like most people, you hate to hear someone, say something derogatory about you and your country. Yes, my remarks will cover the faults of you, as well as Asia and I, the United States and one-hundred and fifty-seven other countries where homelessness, unemployment, under-employed and poverty lives in millions world-wide. This has got to stop. They applauded.

Providers International now has been in eight-countries working on the issues. Today, we are bringing our first-message to a European country. And I will stand before you and say Madrid has a poverty issue, so does Barcelona and four other cities in your country.

I am not proud to say this publicly, but the Country of America has over three-dozen cities with the same issues. "Government don't give a damn about thirty-two percent of the World's population." This must stop and stop soon. More applause.

I spoke for a total of twenty-one-minutes. Then came the biggest surprise of the trip to Spain so far. The Prime Minister stood, left his area and was walking to the stage. The Parliament stood. When he arrived, he shook hands with each of us then walked to the podium.

He thanked us for coming. Both of us thought that the Prime Minister was just being nice. Then he got into his 'cut to the chase' part of his remarks. It is my opinion he said, that the Kingdom of Spain was in need of hearing you; but your messages must be given to the leaders of the cities of the world who have the problems.

The cities involved will ask their government for the help that each community has requested. He turned and was through speaking publicly. Again, we received hand-shakes and he left the stage. His parade-march music started again and he left the theater.

It was our turn to leave and an American Classic came over the sound-system. The music; America, the Beautiful. We left the theater with more applause. I followed Asia out of the door. We were taken immediately to the car and back to the hotel.

"The Prime Minister thinks it is a city issue and that is where the request for money should come from." That might be to our advantage. Moving to Wiesbaden will get us closer to cities than to countries.

We both agreed our speeches were terrific.

In my view it was a complete waste of time spent with the military representative sent from the Navy and the Air Force in Spain. What I got out of it was that they wanted to make their problem our problem. We are not going there. The highest member of the team sent to talk to us was an Air Force major gladder to get off the base then the mission of the visit.

On the international flight going home; the two of us had some fantastic conversation about today, tomorrow and the future. Flying home for a meal, I had what she had going and she had what I had on the trip over. Yes, it's crazy sometimes.

Back in St. Pete the following day at one o'clock we presented our information to the 'big three' plus Della. I think the information we shared about the Prime Minister's remarks didn't go over well; but they agreed the message we sent was well understood and the Prime Minister's remarks were understood as well and will be worked on in the future.

For the next two-days, the primary-conversation at Providers was the topic of Rwanda in Africa. Both Della Faye and Jason are interested and excited for their upcoming travels.

Flights from St. Pete to Orlando, Orland to London, London to Istanbul and finally Istanbul to Kigali.

In 2001, Rwanda was teaching French in schools as the second language in the country. Rwanda is known as the country of one-thousand hills. In 2001 Rwanda was just beginning to grow, and becoming more stable. The country had a government full of terrific leadership.

And their government was anxious for representative of Providers to visit and bring fresh ideas to the country hoping to extend care, educational ideas, the trades opportunity, and help to reduce poverty.

Every place that Providers will go is to fight against and try to reduce poverty. It is a battle for every person to leave the condition poverty represents but it is a topic needed to be fought against world-wide. There are shortages of quality food, employment opportunities, and many educational challenges.

The first to present Provider's case to the Rwandans are Della Faye Sharp and Jason Robert O'Dea. Two beautiful black-people from the inside out and from the outside in. No two better to make the presentation.

I was always a big fan of Nelson Mandela. He has done so much for Africa from his life in South Africa. He has fought to improve poverty and education most of his life. He has stated, "education is a long-walk to freedom."

I have always loved this quote. "Without education your children can never really face the challenges they will meet." Perhaps his most profound. "Education is the most powerful weapon we can use to change the world."

Della and Jason are taking Provider's opinion on both education and poverty to Rwanda to help the country, that I think will be the leader later of counties throughout Africa. May God bless the people of Rwanda. May God bless Della and Jason.

Before the day was over, Mr. Williamson informed us that tomorrow we will have a session on the move to Wiesbaden and what will happen in the mean-time.

The two of us felt glad to be back into our apartments. The two-doors were still open. I believe that will always be the case.

It is getting closer to the time that Della and Jason make their trip to Rwanda. They are going to Kigali, the capital and largest city in the country. Poverty in Kigali in 2001 was seventy-percent below the poverty line. Country wide was near ninety-five percent.

After the genocides and the war of 1994 in Rwanda; thirty-four-percent of the households were ran by widowed women. And throughout the world, women headed households are the most vulnerable.

In the year 2000, Rwanda was the seventh poorest country in the world. In 2000, sixty-percent of the country's population was considered to be in extreme poverty.

Farming has begun helping the poverty level but, in a years-time, the poverty level has only changed by a zero point seven-percent. Most of the crops consist of beans, sweet potatoes, potatoes and the banana crops.

Della and Jason, will meet with government and the city of Kigali people while there.

Flying from Orlando, it will take about eighteen hours to get there. From Orlando to London to Istanbul and finally to Kigali.

The trip was more than an eye opener for both of them plus the company. The first report from Della was gloomy. "Where do I, Jason or the company begin? I personally don't think Rwanda is ready for us and I assure you the company is not ready for Rwanda."

Jason's remarks were gratifying to hear. "I have never met a collective group of nicer people in my entire life." "The people were interested in every word said." "From my perspective, American involvement and a private enterprise or foundation might be ten to twelve-years away in the future." "When the time is right, they will succeed."

"The country needs schools for elementary and secondary education." "The young boys need to grow up and become leaders of men and women alike." "So many men were killed in the genocide; it's hard to believe the numbers."

"In years to come, I don't think there would be a better African nation or literally any nation better to help than Rwanda." "I would bet on it that twenty or twenty-five years from now, Rwanda will be the up-and-coming leading country in Africa."

"I believe that someday an American based Foundation will help the country with education needs and possibly teaching trades as well. When people of other countries see what is going on they will support as well. We can only hope."

Mr. Williamson, was the first to speak. "You two did a marvelous job in country. Your report back was solid and complete. Now, African counties might be the ones to over-look for a decade or so." "Jason, your human approach in your remarks indicate the type of Christian gentleman that you are." "It was great to see and hear."

It was Mr. Carlson who made remarks next. "One trip down and two more very important ones to follow. Our getting ready for our study of

Wiesbaden and the Nightclouds returning to Spain are certainly going to be important for all of us."

CHAPTER THIRTEEN:
THE BOYS ARE BACK

There were five of us in our chairs when Mr. Williamson and Mr. Carlson came into the room. They both said hello to Blake, Della, Jason, Asia and myself. Within two minutes Horatio and Priscilla joined us. They were greeted too.

Soon to join us were his three-top financial guys he spoke about before. Bob Williamson, was excited about the concept of operating a little more than half of our business from Wiesbaden, the Capital of the State of Hesse, in Germany.

"Silas, I congratulate you on your presentation and your wisdom and opportunity you presented." "There are several things we know about Wiesbaden, and more than that we don't know. But we will learn quickly."

"We know there are about two-hundred-ninety-four thousand residing in Wiesbaden and there are about twenty-thousand American military assigned in the area."

"On the human-interest side of affairs; Wiesbaden is one of the oldest-spa-towns in Europe with twenty-six total hot-water springs in the immediate area of the city."

"We are looking in the possibility of renting a series of room either or both of the American Arms Hotel or the Emilia Earhart Hotel." "I want to send, to begin with a two-member research team to Germany to make some assessment and give us some quick-leads and facts so that we can move forward quickly."

"Because Della and Jason just returned from Rwanda, Horatio and Priscilla are just getting here; I am asking officially if Silas and Asia would like to make the trip and do research. I think this is best because Silas brought this possibility forward. Would you two accept?"

Research is one of my favorite hobbies I said. Speaking for myself, I would love to go do the job. Asia said, "I could be packed within the hour." "Apparently." Mr. Williamson said, "You both accept the challenge." "In a New York second." Asia added.

"We are more interested in the American Arms Hotel. It was built in the late 1950's, it is still quite nice and they have mid-range prices on long-term rents." "There are many other things that we will be looking at. I want to have the two of you out of here and in Wiesbaden within a week to ten days." "Is there a reason why you can't?"

Asia asked the question. "Where does this leave us with the Madrid trip and the thoughts of the American military?" "That is water under the bridge long gone down-river."

"Seriously, if it pans out that the Prime Minister of Spain is correct and we are better off talking to cities where we plan to work and help; then that is what we will do."

"Silas and Asia, I want to give you a week to ten days head-start in Hesse before I will come to Germany and review your finding and we together will make some decisions. Speaking of decisions; it will probably be me heading the European group and Mr. Carlson staying in St. Pete. We are both content with that."

"One last question was Lufthansa Airlines the best carrier to Frankfort? I will arrange tickets. It is only twenty-five miles between the two cities."

"Now on one more very important question for the Nightclouds. Would the two of you mind if we sent you to Barcelona, Spain instead of Wiesbaden? In one sense, Priscilla would be going home, both of you speak perfect Spanish, the two of you could see most of the operation in Spain and finally, Horatio could do math and language issues for us from satellite operations." Would you accept that?"

"Certainly." Horatio said. "We will move soon on that subject too. You two will be my eyes and ears in Spain." "Would that work for you?" Again, another certainly.

It is funny how fast a monkey can climb a tree when he sees the fruit on it.

Before we were let go for the day, I brought up a question for Mr. Williamson. I told everyone there still in the meeting that I had a telephone conversation with my dad last evening about the move to Wiesbaden.

He asked me questions that I hadn't thought about and questions that should be answered by you, our leader. My dad volunteered his time to fly to Florida with my step-mom who is also a professor at the University of Idaho.

My dad is a PHD who teaches International Policies and Foreign Affairs. My step-mother is a PHD who teaches Literature. They could fly this Thursday and be here for presentations on Friday, Saturday and Sunday; flying back to Moscow on Monday morning.

His information would come from a five-hundred-level class; the one he teaches to Master Degree candidates. He also said, you can keep my notes.

Mr. Carlson jumped in with the answer. "Immediately tell him yes, Silas, make sure I have the name correct and we will fly your parent's round-trip-first-class." "We would love to hear him speak and enlighten us."

He believes that on Friday there could be a one-hour session followed by questions. On Saturday, two one-hour sessions followed by questions and on Sunday anything we would want to hear again; he would be available.

Mr. Williamson added. "We will also prepare one of our suites for your dad and mom." We were then excused.

On the way back to the apartments Asia commented. "You hadn't told me that." I wanted to surprise you. "Well, you did."

The minute I got in, I called my dad and told him the good news. He said, "we already have the tickets." I told him to cancel them immediately, the company is paying for round-trip-first-class tickets and a suite on the campus here. "Consider it done."

I knocked on my-side of the open doors and the response came back. "Any more surprises." Then I heard her start laughing. How about dinner I asked. "Sure, how should I dress? I just got out of the shower." Now that is trust and faith.

Tuesday and Wednesday were busy, but most of the conversation was about the week-end session. I asked Blake Tate if I could be the one introducing my dad for his first presentation. "Why not."

There were no delays, my parents arrived on time as expected. He called my number and Asia Lynn and I went to their suite on the campus, enjoyed our hugs, conversation and a small snack. My dad had bought Applets in Spokane.

I don't think I had ever introduced my dad to a crowd like this before. It went well. He opened his remarks with a warm greeting to all; telling them he had heard good to wonderful things about the staff.

When he got down to business, he took his own 'Paul Harvey' approach to his presentation. It was time to take notes as you would preparing for the test that would normally follow.

"I want to begin with some information about America very few people understand. Then I will address international matters after that."

"The Supreme Court takes only just above ten-percent of the cases that apply to be heard. Others do not get a hearing." "Is that fair? I don't think so, but it is the rule of the land because the Justices pick and choose which cases they will hear."

"There are some great Lawyers who have never had a chance to argue their case in front of the nine." "For some reasons, the Justices don't care." "You ask the question, 'who gave them that right?' The answer to that question is the Constitution of the United States.

"I tell you this because you might not find fairness in your presentations on an international scale." "I would say that Asia and Silas were fortunate in Madrid because no one there was having a bad day." "Do you know about how many presentations are ruined because the one listening is having one of those days?"

"We are going to learn how to change that." Another example of percentages of positions which are not heard because you must go through multiple layers of government nonsense." "Someone, somewhere is going to keep you from presenting, because they don't like your topic or they are having a bad day."

For what Silas told me that he and Asia went through in Madrid is not out of line in international circles. When the Prime Minister of the Kingdom of Spain spoke his opinion of you have come to the wrong place; you need to talk to the city involved." "Frankly, I agreed with Spain's leader."

"You have to understand that. What you have to say could be better than sliced bread. However, if you can't or are not allowed to talk; who will know that?" "The answer is no body."

"If Provider's has to go through five-layers of government, you will have about a three-percent chance of getting approval." "When you speak one on one with a district, region or city, the percentage is fifty-fifty of getting something done." "With every-layer of conversation you lose fifty-percent of the value at hand."

"I took a few minutes to study Germany and their system. In the State of Hesse, they will completely understand where you are coming from because of the American military's history of being there."

"They are used to seeing Americans every day in their communities." "The State of Hesse will say thank you and we support your cause, but they will also say. Go to Wiesbaden for their participation, action and approval."

"I don't care who you are, my son included, your highway of thoughts might end up on a dirt-road to nowhere." "Furthermore, it wouldn't be your fault." "It doesn't seem fair, but the majority of communities don't and won't care if twenty-five to thirty-percent of their population is at the poverty level."

"Unless you are living it, or you have been above it in the past, or have never got out of poverty; other people don't care." "If they did, governments, states, cities, towns and communities would have done something about it in the past."

"If I was a member of your team, I would be pleased as punch, if we were thirty-percent successful." "Now, I want to get into areas where you become thirty-percent successful or above."

"Mr. Blake Tate: you Sir has been very successful in the selection and hiring of your superior staff. These people believe in you, your company and your mission." "This company needs young, driven HR people to be the first in the region to find out who are those in poverty, how did they get there and what are they capable of doing."

"Example: A man, who is married, has three kids, has been injured, but is soon to be able to get back to work. That is the type of person you need to reach." "Why?" "Because when you bring him out of poverty, you bring four other people with him. One position, reduces poverty by five chairs."

"There will be many countries and cities where there is a great number of former-military who fall under the poverty-line percentages. You instantly realize that former military have been trained before and can certainly be trained again."

"For every percent you bring out of poverty the American national-average is worth two-point-three- people that one job represents." "My suggestion is to have the young HR's study and then go after the persons that will allow more than one to be removed."

"Work your hardest on freeing those who are on the poverty-line based on unexpected circumstances. You will find this client everywhere you look."

"Tomorrow, I will cover the trades, the needs, the requirements, the conditions, and the rewards." "Now, I will take your questions."

Mr. Williamson asked the first question. "When are you going to retire and would you like a position?" Most of us laughed.

Mr. Carlson asked a serious question. "I want to make sure that I understood what you said. You said, as I understand it; that is reaching the go-ahead from thirty-percent or higher of the cities would be an accomplishment." "Does that mean less than thirty-percent is a failure?"

"Mr. Carlson, any percentage that you reach which removes people from any country from below the poverty line is terrific. What my remarks referenced that getting above thirty-percent of the cities to spend money and do their share of the work will be difficult to achieve. Above thirty-percent would be an excellent achievement."

Asia asked. "Avery, what do you believe will be the most difficult portion of any location's presentation?" "I don't want you to think this is a silly answer. I will explain following this statement. The most important element of any of your presentations will be for those listening to take you and the company seriously."

"I say that because they have heard and have known of the problem for years. Now, someone is doing something about it." "It is going to be a tough nut to crack."

Blake Tate wanted to know. "Professor Fox, where would you put most of our financial resources; research or presentation?"

"I think you have to do both and extremely well. Those doing research in an area might come back and say; this could be a waste of time. When they are trained well, listen to them."

"What I am saying from the bottom of my heart is to go for it; and do it now. These are not going to get any better: only worse."

I asked dad, where would you start? "In two places, Wiesbaden and Barcelona. The poverty rate in Germany is fifteen-point-nine percent. In Spain, twenty-point-three percent. The time spent in Africa in Rwanda could open many new doors for you. Time will answer many questions." "You need talented researchers, but you already have some great teams' members."

"Let me add. I would study the possibility of staying only in Spain and Germany." "City after city in both countries are reaching close to twenty-percent of the population under the poverty-line." "Don't overlook Frankfort and or Madrid."

"I am impressed with everything and everyone I have met here." "I salute you all." The questions just kept coming and dad fulfilled his promise; he stayed and answered all of the questions.

"I look for the sessions tomorrow."

Blake pointed out that not to worry about dinner tonight. Provider's is offering a break with a catered BBQ. It will be in the small park across the street from the apartments. Blake added. "There will be some Idaho baked potatoes, and there will be at least one items from each of your states." I hope it is salmon from Washington and not apple pie.

Well, it's time for another session and my father walked to the podium.

"Good morning. I want to start with an old saying." "We would have bacon and eggs, if we had any bacon or if we had some eggs." "I use this because it will be followed in your work to succeed."

"Before you can use the topic of 'trades' you must make sure that if a trade is introduced, there has to be a company of a group of companies that could or would hire those you train. It there is not an opportunity of placement of individual, you have not trade opportunity."

"Let me introduced the topic of needs. You can't teach picking apples in January. The fruit is not on the trees." "If a company tells you they could hire two electricians; don't try to train twenty. There are going to be eighteen who will not be employed."

"Therefore, don't spend good money for a talented trainer of a trade, if the opportunity of placement is not available." "You must know more about those of importance than you need to know about the people who are looking to move up."

"I want you to get the full meaning of the word requirements. If a company tells you that we have such and such. It doesn't mean that they would hire such and such. When the company says we have twenty-working for us; it doesn't mean they would hire ten more."

"Most companies want a client can do more than just walk and talk. When a person is hired, the company benefits because they fill a need.

"Never offer a reward to a company who you have placed someone from your training. If you, do it once, you are a goner." "Everyone will want something for nothing. You can't afford that."

There were only a few questions after the morning session.

When the third and final session began in the afternoon, Avery Fox pulled a fast-one on all of us.

He began the session with, I want my wife Brenda, also a professor at the U of I speak and talk about her background. I will just leave it at that and ask Brenda to come forward.

Brenda Ann Hope Fox began with the following. "You have heard of me as a Literature Professor at Idaho, but there is more than meet the eyes. On the national scene I am recognized as leader of women's rights in Universities and internationally as well."

"There are Foundations I have been connected to over the years. One in Idaho is called: Always Ask. It is not a women's place to be complacent and sit back and do nothing. For a fact, there were many years that it was strictly a man's world. That is not true anymore."

"Always ask, campaigned for women's rights and worked for placement of women in professional positions." "I bring this information to your attention because I don't want to get trapped into a concept of only helping the male client."

"According to facts that Providers have posted. For every one-thousand male you help, there are five-hundred females who get the same assistance." "When you clients are female. They come ninety-percent of the time with children."

"You will be very surprised that the primary reason a woman is in poverty; it comes following a divorce." "A divorced woman could be the best target you could shoot for she has the instant desire to improve her lot in life."

"I know that you have heard much from Avery and I about poverty. Here in America and overseas it is a tangled-mess that in many areas they can't see the bottom of the issues." "As Avery said, 'government won't do anything about it' and cities try to avoid discussion."

"Personally, when Avery spoke of thirty-percent approval figure; I believe that is ten to fifteen points too high." "I wish you success in your endeavor."

When Avery came back to the podium he said. "I asked Brenda to speak because she is very knowledgeable, sincere, understanding and very familiar with poverty in the United States and abroad."

"I want to comment that the corn-field you are going to try to hoe, is long, vast, and bigger than you think. You will bend many an ear, but when it comes to shucking the corn; there won't find many to help."

Dad continued to talk for about another thirty-minutes. He was very thankful he and Brenda were able to speak with us. His remarks were well received.

Now this is where I am coming from. The European Union has talked Euros in 1999. On January 1, 2002 the Euros replaced the Deutschmark in Germany and the Peseta in Spain. The American dollar changed value in those countries in early January. Germany and Spain's currencies slipped again.

Results, the two countries thought that the Euros would gain strength over their original currencies; but actually, lost value initially. Poor countries like Italy and Greece, cause the Euros to fluctuate throughout Europe. When some countries couldn't pay off its debts, other countries like Germany and Spain helped with some of those debt issues.

The country of France had the best transition from Franc's to Euros. The United Kingdom and Denmark did not participate with the Euros and stayed with their own currencies.

CHAPTER FOURTEEN:
HELLO WIESBADEN

Della and Jason's return from Rwanda with the report that they both believed that the African nations were not ready for our company's service. I feel in some ways there is pressure on how Wiesbaden in Germany and also how the Kingdom of Spain will turn out.

I want to point out that Della and Jason gave great accounting of their findings. They have both earned very high-marks in my grade-book for presentation and facts. They make a great team.

Having the trip to Spain behind us, I feel it will make the trip to Wiesbaden easier. I didn't say easy. Both Asia and I have studied long and hard and I feel comfortable that we are both prepared. Doing research for location, property, lodging will be an undertaking but won't have the pressure of meeting a Prime Minister.

The trip through London, Frankfort and then by car to Wiesbaden is only two-days away.

When we packed, we packed mostly casual clothes. Also, winter like clothes as well. Mr. Williamson did book us on Lufthansa Airlines through London to Frankford and by car to the American Arms Hotel.

I told Asia on the plane that one of the first things I am going to eat in Germany are pomp-fries and brots. With mustard made in Germany. "Are they good?" Delicious.

I also told her that I liked the German version of French toast with scramble eggs. For breakfast, I would have black-tea; or German hot chocolate. She told me to stop it. "You are making me hungry."

The ground was damp, but it wasn't raining being driven from the airport in Frankfort to Wiesbaden. We checked in together with adjoining rooms at the American Arms.

The German food vendor was still open outside the front door and out we went for Asia's first pomp fries and a brots. She also loved the mustard.

Yes, there were doors that opened which connected our two rooms. Both of us slept well and long in our own rooms. Breakfast was soon on our agenda and we talked, laughed and looked at each other. That was the best part.

In the hotel in the American Arms was a property-management group which sales or rents houses, business property and company business suites. We loved talking to them and told them that in a week or ten days the big guy would be there but we would like to see some in advance to his arrival.

They needed time to put a series to view together so we set an appointment the day after tomorrow at noon.

I knew what Asia's first question was going to be. "Well, what are we going to do tomorrow?" I spotted a poster behind her on the wall that said enjoy a boat cruise on the Rheine River from Rutesheim to Koblenz.

We were excited to go and a great way to enjoy a nine-hour day with the cruise and great German food. There were stops along the way to view castles and vineyards. I think the cruise was established more for romantic-couples than two business partners. The other will come later I believe.

On the way back down the river, we stayed inside the liner to stay warm and to quietly talk to each other. I forgot to tell you the wine and the sugar cookies were delicious going both ways. It was dark when we got back to the American Arms and sadly, the food vendor was not there. We decided we were not hungry enough to eat.

We got to the management office about ten minutes early and were offered German hot-chocolate to drink. "Thank, you." The officer we spoke with was German but spoke beautiful

English. His name was Wolfgang. When he went to pick up the package that was prepared, Asia said, "That's great, now I am with a Fox and a Wolf." I smiled.

On the road to look at the first property, I realized then when riding in German traffic, look at the passing buildings and not at the highways or streets. We made sure that Wolfgang understood we were only the advanced team and not the decision maker. It was well understood.

I really liked the way that Wolfgang was thinking; the first empty business that was available to purchase was an old-well-kept pavilion that was once a roller-rink. Yes, the inside would have to be divided and made into offices. However, there would be room for product storage and the outside has a big and well-maintained parking area.

The property had been on the market for some time. It already had several rest-room facilities, an area in which they once served hot food and a thinking designer had great latitude in recognizing opportunity.

Asia pointed out; the company could keep a portion of the roller-rink floor for corporate skating and recreation. I told her that I thought it was a very good concept and I thought workable idea.

There were several other positive reasons to think this way. It was an ideal location very close to the autobahn entrance and quite close to a small hotel available for sale as well. It was also only a nine-iron-shot from the Emilia Earhart Hotel.

Again, I told Wolfgang that he had a great mind for property management. He spoke, "you haven't seen anything yet." It is being proven that Asia and I had gone to the right company for this project.

He asked me, "How many offices and the size of most offices do I think the company would need?" The offices would be for at least two executive officer and perhaps six additional nice offices plus plenty of storage space. "I think I have something to show you that might work." "They are asking more money."

We were driven further down-town, quite close to the world-famous Wiesbaden Opera House. This was a nice city park across the street, and I think three German restaurants in the immediate area.

Wolfgang just took us up-town, downtown. The place was all-class and the inside was as plush at the corporate offices in Saint Petersburg. "The building smells of money." Asia said. Wolfgang said it was funny that you would say that. This was a headquarter-building of a financial empire crumbled when their stocks fell in Germany and in Europe. Wolfgang offered, "For the right money it could go quickly."

Asia Lynn asked. "Could we look at the small hotel you talked about earlier today?" "How about we got there now." Wolfgang replied.

The minute we saw the building, my mind immediately started to work. The hotel was about three-minutes walking from the famed Wiesbaden Casino. Holy mackerel, I said. All Asia could say was "wow!"

The building was a German-classic building; built after the Second World War. Just a very short time ago, it had been reinvaded and has a statement on the building: Germany's Finest.

Asia asked. "Why is this building on the market?" Wolfgang didn't hesitate with his answer. "Ownership of this building and business has always been in the hands of one family." "Giant corporations have tried to purchase for years and the family would not budge." "Now, they are not running away; but they are running out of family with the capability of taking on a chore this big."

Wolfgang remarked. "When the family realizes who and for what reason Provider's is coming to Wiesbaden; perhaps they would lower the cost, knowing the value of your goals and direction."

When I saw the five suites on the top floor, I said to Asia. "These could be the corporate offices." She agreed. On the fourth-floor there were three offices and a reception hall that seats two-hundred people.

It would be perfect for full-corporate conferences and large meetings. The reception area on the bottom floor would be perfect for the entrance for clients.

On floors two and three were twenty-four luxury-rooms available for staff and unmarried employees. I don't think there would be room for children and the like.

After the way this afternoon had gone so far, I thought of something that my dad told me years before. "When you work with pros, you get what is professional." So far, Wolfgang has done his job fantastically.

I told Wolfgang that he was not working with a company on a 'beer' budget, but did he have anything that was not so much Champaign? Naturally he said yes. "Should we go look?"

Once we got into the car, Wolfgang asked. "Do we have to stay in Wiesbaden proper?" Why, I asked. "There are other communities around us in the City; which would have additional properties." "Germany has gone through a short-fall recession and there have been businesses who have failed."

Asia answered. "I think we better keep looking here or accept something you have pointed out already. I think Corporate would like to stay in the city."

Wolfgang asked another question. "Would you two like a small afternoon snack? Sure, was the answer. He jumped out of the car and ran into a building. He was back in four minutes.

"Many people in America think you have to have Belgium Chocolates, not me. Germany makes great chocolates too." He turned and handed us a few to choose from. Absolutely delicious.

Wolfgang pointed out that he could take us now for one more to see. It is very close to where the old Lindsey Air Station use to be. "You can't laugh, but it was once an old airplane hangar and has been used for other things since."

The location he said was on the other end of town. Asia responded. "Would most people think we were still down-town in Wiesbaden?" "No, I think not."

I asked Wolfgang if we could see the same products over again in corporate in Florida wanted us to do pictures and measurements? "I have write-up and drawing on everything I have showed you today in the office."

"Let's go back there now and if you would like to fax all of them to Florida; I could do that now and give you two a copy also."

Asia asked if we could write a little cover letter too. "Absolutely."

When we got taken back to the American Arms, we were tired, but satisfied with the first part of the job in Germany. Another tennis line: the ball will soon be in Mr. Williamson's court. I can't wait until after he responds to what was forwarded to him.

Asia received a trans-Atlantic phone call from Mr. Williamson, after the initial greeting asked. "Do the two of you think you have seen enough properties in Wiesbaden to schedule my trip within a day or two?"

Asia answered. "Yes, it you want the property to be in Wiesbaden proper." "We can see the possibilities of each of the properties we looked at and studied. We think it is time for you to come and look for yourself and make some decisions."

I told Asia what my immediate thoughts were. My number one favored piece of property is the small-hotel site. It could hold everything needed others than rooms and I believe the American Arms would do for at least a while.

My second choice would be the former roller-rink which would need a building adjustment, but had many things going for it. When you look at price, they would probably a similar total at the end.

The pavilion is close to the autobahn, close to the American Arms and in an area of town that can be reached easily. The down-side is that it will take a while to do the rebuild.

Asia spoke. "I wonder if the small-hotel group would consider renting the facilities for a guaranteed period of time. Say three-years?" "Silas, do you think that Bob Williamson would consider renting instead of buying?" She continued. "Would Mr. Williamson, think he is taking a risk by buying. Is he dead sure his concept is going to fly?"

Good questions. My phone rang next and it was Williamson that he and Della would be in in two-days: Thursday. They were going to book from Florida, spaces at the American Arms.

"I am glad that Della is coming with him. She has a great mind and would only say what she believed in." "I don't believe in my-heart-of-hearts that she is competing with us. I believe she is our ally."

I suggested tomorrow we should travel the short-distance to Mainz to see the famous Gutenberg printing press. Johann Gutenberg invented the moveable-type printing press in the year 1455. The press and printed pieces of the

Latin Language Bible are made available to purchase.

"That's a wonderful thing to do. I would love it." "Can we find some pomp fries and a brots along the way?" Anything your beautiful heart wants. I couldn't help but tell the warmer her affection, the greater my heart melted. She said, "That's the way it is to be. It is a two-way street. You are not in this by yourself." "Understand?"

I think Asia Lynn hit the nail on the head, when she said. "There are days for us and there are days for Corporate." "If we don't forget that, we will be fine." Agreed, I said.

It was later in the afternoon when Bob and Della arrived at the hotel. They seemed glad to see us. Bob asked. "What are you thinking Silas?" I have several thoughts, but I told the both of them what Asia told you at home a few paragraphs ago. Our favorite choice in the small-beautiful-hotel; if the family would consider us.

"Asia, what about you?" "Within, ten days after closing on the building; we could be hard at it working." "I agree with Silas." I later that afternoon sat up an appointment with Wolfgang for ten in the morning."

In the morning, the four of us were at the management-office five-minutes before the scheduled arrival. We introduced Bob and Della to Wolfgang and Wolfgang introduced Erica to us.

Erica was about forty-years of age, professional, attractive and spoke beautiful Oxford English. She spoke. "I have my college degree from Oxford in England."

Wolfgang carried on as if he was man in charge, but I had my thoughts about Erica. I finally had enough nerve to ask the question. Erica, are you a part of the family that owns the hotel?

"Yes, I am." Now, it was beginning to make sense. Erica was the family member who would say; yes or no to a special deal on the property based on who we were.

In a matter of two-seconds something turned the light-switch on in Asia. She asked the first question; nothing about the property. "Erica, how did you like your studies in England?" "It was splendid." Erica said.

The second-question came immediately from Asia. "Can you tell us what your position is with the family and your hotel?" Her answer was something we needed to know. "I am now the operating-manager and I lead promotion of the property and marketing." "How interesting." Asia said.

It was then we arrived and could see the outside of the building. "This is fantastic." Della remarked. "It is beautiful," Mr. Williamson added. "My family and I think so too."

Due to Asia's questions, the tail is now wagging the dog. Wolfgang is the management-representative, but all of us can speak and hear answers from Erica. Asia continued. "How many years has the hotel been in the hands of your family?"

"Soon after the Second World War when America was still occupying the country." "It was the United States which said you can build the hotel and gave us this property to do so." "As a family we are grateful to the United States."

Bob Williamson asked. "Erica what would you like us to see first?" "How about the top floor and the potential corporate offices?" Mr. Williamson was flabbergasted. He walked over to Erica and gave her a professional hug. She hugged him back." "These are beautiful suites."

I thought I would give both Bob Williamson and Erica something to think about. Erica, would you and your family consider renting the facility on a long-term contract? Williamson looked at me with a puzzled look. His expression changed, when she said; "I could talk to my family about that. Do you mean the whole place?" Probably.

Much to my surprise, Mr. Williamson said. "Let's see how this plays out before we see other properties. I believe Erica is certainly a square-shooter and will do what she says she will do." "I think she has horse power also. She is the one the family sent to examine us."

Wolfgang called my number and said Erica and her family have two possible proposals for Mr. Williamson's review. Could we come by the office at ten in the morning? My answer was yes. I notified the other three and we would be ready and there on time.

Wolfgang was now back in charge as a management-partner. He came in all smiles and sat at the head of the table. He asked Mr. Williamson if he would like a private conversation or could everything be said before all of us.

"I am open to having everyone listening to the concepts involved."

Wolfgang, went ahead with his presentation. He spoke. "The ideas are complete and very simple. Initially it will take a yes or a no answer on each proposal." "Erica was impressed with each of you. She said both Asia and Della could have done her job very easily."

We were told her concept in selling the property would cost one-million dollars. One-half of what her family has put into the business over time. We would own all furniture and belongings.

If we were rented the building and change the interior of the hotel it would cost five-thousand-five hundred a month.

If we rented the facility and did not change the interior as knocking down walls, etc. Her family would love to rent the building and the contents for four-thousand and two-hundred per months. She would have beds removed and leave desks and other furnishings. That would be fifty-thousand, four hundred a year.

Mr. Williamson asked Wolfgang to step out for a while for us to discuss the proposals. When he left, Mr. Williamson asked. "What do you think?"

Asia spoke first. "If we took the last proposal for a three-year period our office costs would be one-hundred-fifty-one thousand, two hundred dollars." "To me that is better than spending a million-dollars buying."

Della spoke second. "The only way I would consider buying was if St. Pete was closed and the entire operation was in Germany." "Interesting Bob said."

Finally, I spoke. I would never at this time consider buying because we are saying the project is going to work. We are willing to give it a try for three-years. If it does work to a tee, it could be purchased later. I would not spend more than five-thousand a month and give it a try.

I want to add one more thing. Erica, was good to her word. She talked to her family and the asking values were greatly lowered.

Mr. Williamson began. "What if I didn't like any one of the concepts?"

I said, I think you are missing the boat. She is giving us a great opportunity. Then Mr. Williamson said, "what if I wanted to buy?" Asia said. "I think you would be taking a risk." "What do you think Della?" "I agree with Asia, you would be at risk."

"I have made a decision. I would like to be able to modify the building. I would pay sixty-six thousand a year. In three-years that would cost one-hundred and ninety-eight thousand. Far cheaper than a million-dollars." "Do you all agree?"

Della the business leader asked. "How and why did you make your decision so quickly?" His answer. "Silas and Asia did my home-work for me." "Bring Wolfgang back in here."

"Wolfgang, you can report to Erica that we will take the 'can modify' rental agreement and for you to prepare the documents." "Mr. Williamson, why don't you tell her yourself?" "She is here in the office." "I would love too, Bob said."

When Erica came into the office, we all stood and thanked her for her kindness and that of her family. Then came the surprise from Mr. Williamson. "Erica, when this is completed; will you be looking for an employment opportunity?"

"I would love to have you come work for us. It has nothing to do with the arrangement. It has to do with the qualities you represent. You would work with the three around the table?"

"I think I can arrange that." Asia added. "Would you like to come to America for a couple of weeks to learn about the process?" "Yes, I would like that. When will we leave? When Wolfgang says the process is complete." "We all want to stay and play in Germany for a few days until this mission is complete."

Before leaving the office, Wolfgang told Mr. Williamson. "You don't have a staff; you have a Board of Directors." That was the nicest thing I heard all day.

When we got back to the hotel, Mr. Williamson explained why he offered Erica a position. "She is familiar with the building, the city, the German government, her working staff, the underemployed, the unemployed in Germany, the poverty and the city of Wiesbaden. She would be an instant, knowledgeable, member of the staff."

I think we all agreed with Bob. It took three-days to put the package together. Provider's will begin paying rent and move the American people to Europe in early January. By January 20, 2002 we should be close to operational.

We all flew back home on Lufthansa, including Erica, and we were home a few days before Thanksgiving 2001. On the day of 'Thanks' I had different emotions going through my mind.

Nine-eleven was still bouncing off my inner walls, moving to Germany was going to happen, and probably nine more topics.

It seemed like Della, Asia, Jason and myself were working for Bob Williamson now. However, we knew that Blake Tate would be in Wiesbaden with us. Erica, settled in quickly and instantly proved how talented she was. It was a great hire. As a matter of fact, I hadn't seen anyone at Providers who wasn't a great hire.

As we made our way toward Christmas, progress was being made and we were looking forward to a company dinner and a presentation by Mr. Williamson on December fifteen. I would guess the presentation will be on Saint Pete, Wiesbaden, Germany and Barcelona, Spain.

There was a memo that circulated today indicating that by February first, Barcelona should well be on the way. Staffing had to be completed by then to match the timeline.

CHAPTER FIFTEEN:
KNOWING WHAT'S UP

On December fifteenth, the staff was tired but ready for the evening. I was in a suit for the first time in three-weeks. Asia was dressed lovely as were all of the people.

It was a nice meal but people were more interested in the festivities and the fire-works to follow. I asked Asia if she expected any surprises. "I think there will be several items we don't expect. Surprises, I am not so sure about." I didn't agree with Asia's assessment. I think something are going to hit the fan. I don't think all people are going where you think they were going.

When Bob Williamson walked to the podium, there was applause, but no vocal comments. "Good evening." He started with, "Merry Christmas and I hope you are ready, prepared and excited about the New Year to come." "The company is looking forward to what is next to achieve."

He back tracked for a couple of lines when he said the trip to Germany was a major success and the transfer to Barcelona is on schedule and doing well. And then he said it was time to get to the heart of the matter. You could have heard a pin-drop, dead silence in the room.

"I have studied this issue of the move with inside and outside the office personnel. I have asked opinions of quality-in-house personnel." "Mr. Carlson and I have kicked the can down the road. Sometimes in different directions to make sure we are positive in what we are planning to do."

"We have so much talent in this room this evening; it amazes me how much quality is here." "Mr. Carlson and I have put needs in front of opinions in some categories and reversed it in others."

"In what I am about to tell you and ask you to do could have some surprises for some. To Carlson and myself, these are improvements, achievements and in some cases promotions in duty."

"The homework we have gone through points out in the end; Africa is not ready for us. The Med is not calling to us, but the biggest areas are with the allies of America and the governments we have worked with in the past the most."

"The two countries we are going to work with first are Germany and Spain. No surprise there." "There is one surprise in Spain. We are going to operate out of Barcelona instead of Madrid. In Germany it will be Wiesbaden instead of Berlin or

Frankfort or other places." "We were delighted with the advantages found in Wiesbaden."

"There is a surprise in this next announcement. Blake Tate and his assistant Louise and Horatio and Priscilla Nightcloud will spear-head operations in Spain." "I thought we needed a proven HR Director in Barcelona for hiring purposes." "Horatio will be involved with most of the operation, including day-to-day planning and necessity." "He will be a Chief Executive Officer." There was some applause.

"It is Mr. Carlson's and my opinion, that Wiesbaden will become the company's center of operation; at least for the time being." "I will take my title of President with me to Wiesbaden. Erica House, a German hire, will be the new Chief of Staff, in Germany. Della Sharp will be the Director of Administration, and Jason O'Dea will be the Director of Public Affairs." More applause.

"We will have two Chief Executive Officers, Asia Dash and Silas Fox. Both are promotions." The attendees were now standing and applauding. "They will get into the nitty-gritty of what we are doing in Europe."

"Another surprise, Katarina Damaris, will be our in-house Director of Security and will be traveling in the hip-pocket of our execs as they travel in Europe" Much louder applause.

"Perhaps are greatest challenge now being to hire necessary positions for both Wiesbaden and Barcelona. People we have working in St. Pete who are interested in traveling will have first-opportunity. For the next month, Blake Tate will be the point-of-contact."

"I want to conclude my remarks with the following: we are moving forward, by shaking the place up a bit; but with great anticipation and excitement. If we continue to be one-family with one direction; we will not fail." He was given a longstanding ovation.

In our first meeting on Wiesbaden, Williamson asked Erica House to speak on knowledge of Wiesbaden. We were all ready with note-pads. Erica, is a pretty blond with dark eyes, professional but not flashy. She has a very strong presents but a soft-voice and a sincere smile.

Erica opened her remarks with a smile and some humor. "Would you like my comments in English, German or French?" "Okay, English it is."

"My first challenge Mr. Williamson hit me with was for me to speak on any topic I wanted as long as it dealt with poverty involving German people." "I have prepared that."

"In Wiesbaden proper, there is not a situation where you can say, 'on the other side of the tracks. Poverty is not that simple in Germany. Nearly every street could have wealthy or poor only a few houses apart."

"This is how I would suggest reaching the people. I would recommend advertising the possibility of assisting people under the poverty line." "The advertising could be done through newspaper stories, bulletin-board posters, billboards and other means." "The company needs to be introduced to Germany in as many ways as possible."

"We would instruct how the people register and accept one-hundred and fifty people from the poverty level at a time; and invite them to our building and use the hall on the four floor to have them complete paper-work with their history and to listen to Asia and Silas on how and why are system works." "If necessary, we would use a German translator."

"What we learn from their input on paper will determine our means of helping." "We must be well schooled in doing what is right the first time without errors or mistakes." We will have their phone-numbers and/or addresses for contacting them again." "We can use this system day-after-day reaching potential candidates."

"In a two-week period, we should reach a total of fifteen-hundred people; men and women both." "Our primary concern is how quickly we could reach and help these people." "Our original survey will answer that question. We will find out if they are skilled, have been left-off of work or are at the start line for employment." "We need quality people to recognize the needs."

"At the same time, we will be reaching out to Wiesbaden businesses from large companies to mom-and-pop stores or shops. We become a finding service for these people."

"Since our announcement about Wiesbaden, five cities have approached us. They include Mainz, Stuttgart, Nuremberg, Mannheim and Heidelberg." "We are just scratching the surface. I don't think we are ready to hammer the big guys yet."

If there are companies who are looking for people in a variety of trades. We will find trainers, teachers and leaders of those trades needed." "This is much different than finding people living under bridges and asking them can we help." "Our success will come from people who come to us for a hand-up, not a hand-out."

"I believe that our people like Della, Jason, Asia, Silas and myself within a three-month period can and will reach and assist close to one-thousand people. At that total we would be successful, but it would take us years to solve the majority of the poverty crisis in Germany. But by saving one, is an achievement."

"I think we already have the staff we need in our Public Affairs person, our administrator and our presenters." "I truly believe, all we need is time and the proper preparation and the highway to pass our information to those in need." "I will use a line from Silas. In my military mind I think we can do this."

I raised my hand to ask Erica a question. "Yes, she said." I asked her if we could hear the information again in French. She smiled, "pas de probleme; no problem."

On a serious note; I asked her if she thought this system would work in Spain.

"I think that Blake will have to test the process. We could find a location to hold this presentation that Horatio and Priscilla could give." "I recommend we study the question." "Horatio and Priscilla speak the Spanish language."

There was not a soul at the meeting that didn't agree with Erica. She certainly qualifies as a Chief Executive Officer. Asia said. "I think she is gifted." Della commented. "I am glad that Erica wasn't in charge when the War was going on. She is smart as a whip." I added, sharp as a tack.

The next few days, Williamson, Carlson, Tate, Louise, Horatio and Priscilla huddled and began the hard work of finding the staff for Barcelona.

Several people from the current staff in St. Pete have shown areas of interest in going overseas.

It was good to learn from Blake Tate that under current monies and staff requirements, the company could have as many as eighty-eight total employees. I asked Blake, how many of the people working in the other eight countries could or would want to work in Spain or Germany? "I would imagine, most would want to do so."

Then I asked, what is the timeline in the other countries and how close are they to concluding. Mr. Williamson heard the question and he jumped in to answer. "Maybe, we don't need to complete any more projects in those countries; maybe they are the answers to personnel shortages in Spain and maybe Germany. Good thinking Silas."

It was Asia who said to Della. "Do you have a handle on who is where and what backgrounds are involved?" "Yes, we know exactly.

My thought would be we could keep our oriental teams in some countries and bring other teams with skills to fill many of our needs. I believe we would have at least a dozen we could move." "I will give you specifics within two hours."

I thought back a few days to when Wolfgang told Mr. Williamson that he didn't have a staff but a board of directors. There is not one dense person in this company. All are sharp, smart and 'electric' thinking in this group.

Horatio asked if he got to endorse any of these people for Spain. Tate answered. "Yes, every one of the members on your staff." Horatio, then said something to Priscilla in Spanish. They both laughed as did one of the members of the St. Pete group. Horatio was there in a flash. "Do you speak Spanish?" "Se," he said. "I have found one for Spain." Horatio remarked.

It seemed collectively; we were not working. However, getting a bunch of things done. Williamson, sat up-front smiling. He must have thought the same as I did.

The reign in Spain was not falling on the plain. It would soon fall on the shoulders of Tate and the Nightclouds.

Asia and I got waved at and Bob Williamson wanted us to follow him to his office. When we got there, he invited into his office and told us to get comfortable. "I want to pick your brains." "I want honest opinions and regardless of what you say; you won't be stepping on any body's toes. Understood?"

"Asia, what about manning in Spain. What and how would you do it?" "To start with I would bring the dozen here to St. Pete that Della thought she could remove from the other countries."

"Silas, same question?" "Bob, I would bring all twenty-eight the company has in the eight countries and fill as many holes in one swoop. Take the 'time-out' that is needed, when you pick the crew, return others not chosen to where they were.

Forget about the fact that some are oriental, Latino, black, white and whomever. Spain is a melting-pot like the US; I wouldn't keep anyone out of Spain because of race, creed or background.

Our major victories are going to come from Europe and maybe the Med. I wouldn't place manpower in areas where the most important areas go short. You are the man-in-charge; all you have to do is pull the trigger and the game begins.

"Asia, is he always like this?" "Yes, most of the time." "Does he ever ask your opinions?" "Ninety-percent of the time."

"Let's go find Blake Tate, I am going to pull the trigger and bring everyone back to St. Pete for consideration." "Those in St. Pete who looked into going to Europe will get top-preference."

We were following Mr. Williamson, out of the executive area and walking. I realized Asia was holding my hand. I squeeze it hard for her to get the message.

Bob Williamson called about a dozen of us together. Myself, Asia, Tate, Jason, Della, Horatio,

Priscilla, Carlson, and four others who wanted to be transferred to Spain.

Maybe finding people for Barcelona will be easier than I thought. I am anxious to hear what and how he says it. "I just spent about thirty-minutes with two from my 'think-tank', I have finalized my thinking on positions for Spain.

"At this time, we know that we now have secured four persons going to Spain: the two Nightclouds, Tate and Louise. We know their positions and we think we have outlined the other needs; we will have either eighteen or twenty-people working in country.

Therefore, we have four from St. Pete who would like to go, twenty-eight coming in for evaluation. We have sixteen position to fill from thirty-two candidates." "I think we can do this." "If Blake and or Horatio want the candidate for a position, if they pass our security-check; I will sign-on without any questions."

"As far as the eight-other countries; we will play the process by the seat of our pants until things can be made permanent."

Asia, I have a thought. "Oh boy, here we go again." "What is it?" Do you think it is possible that you and I will be asked to go to Barcelona to look for property?" "Wow!"

We nailed Wiesbaden in five days. We could do Spain in a week. "I am ready if you are?"

CHAPTER SIXTEEN:
YOU MEAN BARCELONA?

Mr. Williamson was having a great day and he wasn't going to stop. "I want to see Asia, Silas, Della, Jason and Erica now. My office will be fine." There was no question at all now as to who we all are working for: Bob Williamson.

We gathered and were sitting in his office. "I have a major project, that I don't think I have to write it; only to approve of it."

"I want it named: The Wisdom of Wiesbaden." "It should include every angle including security. At least one-paragraph per topic." "You got two-days to give me a draft."

"This is how it is going to go down. Asia, you create the topics and don't leave anything out. Della, you outline the needs of administration. Jason, you outline public affairs, Erica, you oversee submissions and Silas, you are my editor and it must be the best stuff you have done to date here."

"Note: At one time or another; all of you will take the lead. Before the draft comes to me, all five of you must indorse the paper before it is processed." "Asia, by the way, you must outline all topics that are not covered by others." "Anyone here in St. Pete can and should be a resource of information." "Give it to me in a nutshell."

The final draft: nutshell presentation.

THE WISDOM OF WIESBADEN – Opens a permanent headquarters in Europe. It represents a central location in Europe and our targets cities are reachable in just a matter of hours. Our cost index is favorable. Allows us to work in warp-speed.

STRUCTURE – Our structure is identified with and by sound reasoning. It is established and anchored by professional staff members, who are appreciated and accepted within their roles with the company. The company is deemed ready for achievement. Everything is in place.

MANAGEMENT – The management team and staff are seasoned professional; highly skilled, competent, and competitive. There are no rocks that are not turned over and looked under. No surprises only professionalism.

ADMINISTRATION – The best organized ever. Director and staff are well schooled, proven, sharp and dependable. The staff has walked the walk; and talked the talk. There are no rookies here.

BUDGET-FINANCE – Staff is polished, full of knowledge and the company is financially stable. Goals are obtainable, achievable and well supplied. The objective will be met in and on time in the near future.

SECURITY – Safety is the first responsibility. Company is well protected and is constantly being trained. Former American FBI agent to lead the cause.

DIPLOMACY – Understood, is followed and proven. Always practiced.

PUBLIC POLICY – The purpose of being in Europe. Well studied.

BUSINESS PLAN – A Combination of Above Articles

CONCLUSION – The House is in Order

It was announced a short time ago by the executive staff that Katarina Grace Damaris will be in St. Pete tomorrow. She is looking forward to being in Germany and keeping us all safe. I can hear what she will say again when she arrives. "The house will come to order." She is a kick in the pants, it is going to be fun.

I'm thinking about doing a short-timers calendar for the Wiesbaden crowd. I am beginning to wonder if we have to send to ourselves in advance of going a 'care' package of additional clothes and supplies. I just might have to give up one of my suitcases just for some of Asia's clothes.

"Could you two handle another job? I am thinking we need an activities calendar and a count-down calendar for Wiesbaden." "Do you have any ideas?" Asia said. "I was thinking about us preparing individually what's needed, but have an international carrier pick up here at corporate. They could do their own container packing." "In the military it was called 'hold-baggage'?"

Then Williamson asked me. I spoke. Let's identify all who are going on the first trip. Asia and I can talk to each, establish a time for having their first shipment ready and brought here for packing. We also need to include in the first packing all of the office material we think will be needed.

This is who I think are going to Wiesbaden. Mr. and Mrs. Williamson, Asia and I, Della and Jason, and Erica House. My question is how many support people are going up-front?

"Yet to be determined." Williamson said. "I hope I can have that for you tomorrow." I think we need two secretaries, two stenos and a couple of runners capable of anything. We need to identify them by name.

Maybe, we don't have to take anyone with us. Perhaps, some of Erica's staff could fill in? I am getting smarter every day.

I did not confer with Williamson, but I did ask Erica about her recommendation about her staff in Wiesbaden. "I would say about five, I would recommend. Three for the reception area and two where needed. All five speak excellent English."

I called Williamson's secretary and asked if there was a chance to see him for a couple of minutes. She said, "Come over now and I will get you in." I did and she did.

He opened the door when I knocked. "Erica has called and I said go for all five." "Because of Erica's blessing we can do that for Wiesbaden and not able to do it yet in Barcelona." I told him thank you and headed back to my office and my preparation.

Within five minutes my phone rang. Williamson asked me to grab Asia and come by his office for he forgot to ask us a question. So, I did.

He began his remarks by saying that I believe the two of you have about ten days when you don't have anything special on your calendar. "Do you have an idea what I want to ask the two of you?"

"Asia answered. You want us to go to Barcelona and find a property and housing solution." I was surprised at his answer. "No, but that is a hell of an idea." "Would you consider doing it?"

I asked. What was the reason for inviting us over now? "I wanted you to look into how the hiring process was going for Barcelona and if we saw any flaws in what was happening."

I looked at Asia when she spoke. "When would you like us to fly to Barcelona?" "Day after tomorrow." "You got to get packed."

I asked, will you be coming to review our process and finalize it? "No, I think you two can do it. I'm busy."

When leaving his office, I asked Asia if she put the wagon in front of the horse. "No, we don't have wagons and horses; we deal with tractors." Oh, I said. How did she come up with tractors?

From tractors to fact. Barcelona, or anywhere in Spain; is not going to be a piece of cake. It will be like a pain in the butt. When Della and Jason told us of Rwanda; perhaps Spain might be like that too. The people or the situation is just not right yet.

CHAPTER SEVENTEEN:
THE PAIN IN SPAIN

It is going to be at least a week before the twenty-eight-people to headquarters from the eight countries get here. Transportation is not easy from out of the way spots. The interviews will start when all people have arrived, and are cleared and are safe.

The story of Barcelona is not a good one when it comes to poverty. A total of twenty-six-point one percent of the people fall into the category. Four out of ten family with children live on less than thirteen-hundred euros' per-month.

There are two main languages in Barcelona; Catalan and Spanish. About fifty-fifty in the population. In the poorest district in Barcelona: Can Pesquera, more people speak Catalan.

Barcelona is on the Northeast corner of Spain located on the Mediterranean Sea. It is the highest city on the Med. It is the second largest city in Spain and has close to one-point-three million population. The beaches in Barcelona are artificial and were built, for the Olympics in 1992.

It is hard to believe but the city is older than Rome. It is the world most famous for bikes and pedestrian streets in Europe. It is the most visited city in Spain; almost twice as many per year than Madrid.

There are fifty-six parks in the city, the largest one in the world is located there. There are fifty-five museums. Barcelona is known for its architecture and culture. But close to forty-percent of the people there don't celebrate in its culture. In all of the European cities, Barcelona is known for the city of people who have; and people who have not.

Most of the homes for the have nots; are self-made.

I have done some further studies and I have located two-hundred and twelve corporate properties available in Barcelona. They come in all sizes and shapes and through the city. In Wiesbaden we only looked at five-potential locations but we were told there were more than one-hundred. Germany will turn out fine.

In my study I found one-fact almost impossible to believe. In all of Barcelona's rentals; nearly ninety-percent of the hotel renters are visitors to the city and seventy-one percent of the visitors to the city come from outside of Spain.

Asia asked. "Are you sure you want to do this?" Do we have a choice? "Probably not." "But I know, we will do a great job."

We had a further conversation with Bob Williamson. "What type of rental budget do we have for Barcelona? "Try to keep it about one-hundred-twenty-five thousand a year." Two or three years? "Probably two-years." "How many people do you believe will be assigned there? "Certainly not more than a dozen."

His last answered told for me how important Wiesbaden was going to be in comparison to Barcelona. I was trying to get a handle on types of potential sites. Asia threw a curve at me that I hadn't thought about; but I loved. "What about an old school with two or three separate buildings?"

From Orlando we had to fly to London and then hop over to Barcelona. We flew on United to Europe. Very nice, but not the best. Before we left home, we were given a location to stay in Barcelona and a management company to contact.

The hotel was nice and the management contact called himself Sidney. He had a Spanish name but none of us could be able to pronounce it. I asked myself; where is Priscilla?

We gave Sidney our documents and our line of finance documents and we were ready to do business. Asia told him that we didn't really have much time to look or barter for costs. "Let's see your best property up front." I mentioned, we might be interested to see office space as well as living quarters.

I found out that Sidney and our friend Wolfgang in Germany were a lot alike. Sidney, very well could have been the nicer man to do business with. He wanted to know if the office should be furnished and how many offices in total?

I told him four executive suites and perhaps as many as eight other nice and comfortable spaces. He said he could handle that. He said he had a location in mind; ten-minutes to the city center by walking and up-town in quality.

If you didn't like to look at the driving in Wiesbaden; you didn't want to look out at the buildings on the side of the streets. No, you wanted to close your eyes and maybe even pray. It would take some time to get used to it.

He said we are here. We are in the section of the city known as Eixample. The place was perfect. Three executive suites and nine lovely support-staff high quality. More than splendid. How about the rental cost per month, per year, per two years, and three years? Also, would it come furnished?

Furnished the cost would be four-thousand-three-hundred and thirty-three US dollars per month. That would be fifty-one thousand nine-hundred and ninety-six thousand per year. Price would be guaranteed for two years.

Asia said. "We could live with that. Now, how about the quarters for twelve people?" Sidney spoke. "I have something in mind about four American blocks away. A former hotel made into individual apartments." "I think I could house all twelve for six-thousand US dollars a month. Seventy-two thousand a year. Same price for both years."

Could you show us the apartments? "Let's go now." Both of us liked what we saw. Nice but not swanky. The kitchens in each had everything. The bedroom was a little small but typical European.

So, I said to Sidney. For less than one-hundred and twenty-five thousand a year we could get the offices and the housing? "Yes, to be exact; One-hundred and twenty-three thousand, nine hundred and ninety-six dollars per year."

Do you have pictures and write-ups on both in which we could forward to our home office in Saint Petersburg in Florida, USA? "Certainly, you could write a cover letter too."

Let's us go back to your office and do that. Asia said, "I love two-stop shopping." Me too, especially in Barcelona, Spain.

The answer came back from Bob Williamson within two-hours. "Go for it." Two days later the papers were signed and we were on our way home.

When we arrived home, we were considered conquering heroes. Our job was now done and we were back in the Wiesbaden mode with one-week left to go before we traveled again.

Asia asked. "Do they pay us enough money?" They pay what we agreed too. "Stupid us." Yep!

Asia and I told the primary four headed to Barcelona that we felt Spain in general was going to be very difficult. Our opinion was that we could train, teach and develop; but there were no one ready to hire or inspire in any fashion.

We had a meeting with Bob Williamson and told him of potential issues we have found. Barcelona is dying; but not dead yet. We will soon have to have a round-table discussion. If we have to cut our losses and run' it is best to do that up-front in broad daylight.

CHAPTER EIGHTEEN: *MANY FOXES*

When Katarina Grace Damaris arrived on campus, the only woman missing was Savannah Jade, who was still helping Alan with his recovery in San Antonio. With the addition of Erica, Louise, Della and Asia; the girls were back in town.

Katarina brought with her some bad news from Texas. The doctors have told Alan even with surgery; he would always have to use a cane to walk the rest of his life. The All-American was done running. Kat also said that Savannah was through running also; she was finding a home with Alan in San Antonne.

Katarina said "they will never be with Providers." "But thank God, I am." Katarina, let the 'real' Kat out of the bag. My partner was severely injured and the gun-shot really did damage to his shoulder. Serving the country, he was defined as a great FBI agent and had received many accolades before his injury.

Going from a 'top gun' to removed was almost too much for him to take. I think in time he will recover." "He is being treated for a healthy mind in Portland, Oregon. "Before I left the agency in

Seattle, I was given a briefing on Germany. It, was like a going away present."

"Germany's open borders issues has caused the country to be less safe now than in the past." "I was going to tell the company about this if I was going to join you again or not." "The Germany government has had open borders for a little over a year and the bad of the world has gathered there and has brought the evil with them."

"Frankfort, Berlin and the bigger cities are being over ran by hoods with guns, drugs, prostitutes and the like." "Your jobs have to go on, but with care and concern."

"None of what I am going to show you is loaded. But I want you to watch." From out of her lower back under her jacket, she pulled a pistol. Nice, I thought. From what appeared to be a false pocket from her slacks; came a small hand-gun. Without a moments-notice was a hand pistol from just below the knee on her left leg. I was amazed.

She smiled and spoke again. "I am now presently licensed to carry concealed weapons aboard flights, in Europe and I will be informed of the strength of the weapons when in city of Wiesbaden which will be allowed to be carried." "But I will be to be close by when we are out and about."

"I would suggest that your mission being carried out from mid-morning to early afternoon.

Late afternoon and evening are usually the troubled times." "I have told Mr. Williamson, that I won't travel with you, but you won't be out of my sight."

"I also told Bob that I have a female friend of the FBI that would be available in the future if needed." "She is a phone call and a couple of airplane rides away." "She is the Jill that carries all of the 'Jack' everywhere she goes. By the way, she outscored me on the last range test I had." "We are known as 'salt and pepper'. Yes, she is black."

"I guess my message is over. But the time amongst my friends has just begun again. My job is to keep you safe and I will."

Erica stood and asked to speak. "Everything that Katarina just said about Germany is the truth and all of the good German people know it." "I am glad Kat is with us and I feel safer with her on our side."

That was a spontaneous message from a woman from the city of Wiesbaden. The program will go on, but under protection and caution. Kat then added addition words. "I would like to live in the room on the third floor closest to the elevator." "So be it." Mr. Williamson said.

When I was listening to Katarina this idea came across my mind. We need two more directors in Wiesbaden. Why could they not be Katarina and Jill at three-quarter time directors and twenty-five per center of their time be security. I need to send a message to Williamson.

He is looking into it. I just got the word. Jill St. Cloud, is going to be asked to join us permanently.

The next subject to be discussed was the early shipment of personal and personnel materials and luggage. It will be sent in three days.

The early shipment was well thought out. Plenty of product for all of us and necessary clothes for all of us. Providers loved to use the DHL Company for shipments to Europe. The shipment is flying two days before we are. It will be there when we get there.

I went over my notes again about Wiesbaden. Germany is different than most countries. In Germany the economy and those with some money are mixed in with daily activities where some people with a few Euros who are trying to live with people who are quite well off.

The majority of persons living in Germany under the poverty line are people who are underemployed than those out of work. Companies kept many people on their payroll, but often time's people were asked to take a small pay cut and keep their jobs.

Most people at the time of depression choose to keep their jobs instead of being unemployed. Many companies would rehire people who previously lost income to return to the level of income they once had. Therefore, the overview of the situation was that the companies were trying to make their entire staff above the poverty line but were not hiring from the outside.

Because of this the people of Wiesbaden and elsewhere in Germany were allowing the 'haves' to keep working and the 'have nots' on the street unemployed. The economy in Germany is not a pretty site.

Lastly, the gap between the employed and the unemployed has grown much wider. There are worthy men and women in Germany who would be easy to train with a trade; but seldom is a trade being hired.

We are going to take on the concept of a handful at a time. In all honesty, Wiesbaden looks like a ballgame; Barcelona looks like a rain-out.

CHAPTER NINETEEN:
SOON TO BE IN EUROPE

We all were on the same Lufthansa flight. The Williamson's were the only two flying first class. The rest of us were in the back of the plane; Asia and I were in the very back row; if it were a car, we would be on the passenger side.

It was ideal for us, close to the galley, food, snacks and the rest rooms. A short walk down the aisle. Asia asked. "Are you ready for one-more-go-around?" I said, I think we had to be.

Before we left Saint Pete, I asked Mr. Williamson if Asia and I could have the adjoining rooms furthest from the elevator on the third-floor. "Why would you want to do that," he asked? Much less noise in the hall-way. "The room are yours."

Asia Lynn was returning to Germany, a country in her initial application said that she liked. My thoughts of Germany were that I really loved the time spent in Mainz and the travels on the Rhine. And I can't forget the pomp fries and the brots.

The concept I had pertaining to the rooms was, would there be enough closet space for clothes? I think that my sweaters will have to be folded and put in drawers. I think we might have to hang clothes by seasons of the year.

The flight was uneventful. We rented a bus from Frankfort to Wiesbaden with the back full of luggage, had much conversation and excitement from everyone. Moving in was project number one.

My room was the last one on the third floor on the right side of the hallway. Asia's Lynn's room was next to mine. Della was next to Asia, and next to Della was Jason O'Dea. The Williamson's took the first two rooms off of the elevator the right side of the hallway. Katarina and Jill were the first off of the elevator on the left side. Erica also had a room designated to her on the third floor, but would spend most of her time with her German family.

The two German men hired would be staying also with their family in Wiesbaden.

Karl Muller, for the hotel was chief of building security. He will maintain that position. Hans Schultz, was the chief of maintenance, made repairs and maintained quality assurance that all was in good working order. He will remain as such.

The three women hired will be roomed on the third floor. Ursula Wagner, will remain as the company's secretary for Bob Williamson and

Erica. She speaks three languages. German, French and English.

Sara Weber, she did all of the ordering for the hotel and she will remain in purchasing. She also speaks multiple languages. Emily Fischer, will remain as the company's primary greeter. She is well schooled and can write and speak three languages. They all will be helpful.

The executive office suites will go to Bob Williamson, Erica and Della. Other offices will house: Asia, myself, Jason, Ursula, Katarina, Jill, and Karl Muller. The main floor offices will have Hans, Sara and Emily.

We were right about space for hanging clothes. The company might have to buy ward-robe chests.

I have never seen a more talented line-up and that includes the recent baseball line-up of the New (Hatem) York Yankees.

I just got word that at five o'clock this evening; in about two hours; Bob Williamson is going to have introduction of the German hires and a quick meeting to set the foundation of our first company mission in Germany.

I am assuming it deal with the first initial advertising of our poverty campaign.

The meeting is going to be on the fourth floor in the theater. Asia asked me the question. "Do you remember how to get to the auditorium?" No, not really but we will find it.

My question for Asia Lynn was; what do you think they are going to do with the dozen rooms on the second floor? "Maybe we can put tables in them and have them be the place where applicants fill-out paperwork." "They could also become classrooms for trades teaching." I told her she was smart as a whip. She replied. "You're right."

"What do you think they could be used for?" My answer was two or three could be used for storage. "You're pretty sharp too."

It was fun listening to Erica and Bob introduce the five-new hires. They were all very bright, sharp and professional. Each had a chance to speak. Hans, immediately reached me. "Give me a list of what are your needs beyond what was brought with you. They will take two of three days to acquire."

I had a chance to talk with Bob and Erica about our first opportunity in Germany. This is how the conversation went. I reminded the two of them that the hotel has a four-chair barber-shop and a four-chair beauty-shop on the first floor.

Our first advertising should include positions for unemployed or underemployed barbers and beauticians. The reason, if we expect to place people in the business world, they must look fresh and clean.

I recommended that we look for ten each barber and beauticians. The reason being having two day shifts from eight to one and the second from one until six. We should also have support personnel who will do shampoos and other positions.

Also, in our first hire or look to hire we need about four people who could handle the laundry facility in the building. Primarily able to do towels and sheets and personal laundries. Dry cleaning for the employees will be sent out.

Erica smiled right away and said, "You have been thinking again." Bob was looking for clarity when he said, "the barbers and beauticians would be doing hair of those coming out of poverty; basically, looking for employment with a clean fresh look." "That's a great idea."

Initially, we would be the employer of the health and beauty department. But soon on the second and additional haircuts; there were then be a small cost. I suggest free haircuts in the morning, cost in the afternoon by appointments.

To begin with those brought in would have their own hair done by other barbers and beauticians. I guess we could find some thirty-to-forty applicants on our first publication.

The first publication went out and we had thirty-one contact us within seven days. Seventeen current or former barbers, ten beauticians and four who are doing or have done shampoos, etc.

Hans donated products arrived with the fresh new equipment and within another week we were ready to start the process. Several of the ten beauticians came from underemployed positions. They were well qualified. Four of the beauticians were graduates of beauty-schools but were not working at the time.

Of the seventeen who said they were barbers, only fourteen actually were. Three were looking for work. I told the 'big guy' upstairs maybe a couple of the three could learn to do the laundry detail. "Good idea."

I was the first of the employed at Providers to jump into a chair and got my hair trimmed. The barber did a great job. By the time the training process was over and the eight barbers and two cashiers were selected; all of the guys have had our hair cut; thanks to the company.

From the women's side of things, Ursula, Sara, Emily, Erica, Asia, Katarina, Jill, and Della went through the works. The staff from the women's side was easy to select. Once the team was set; even Mrs. Williamson jumped in and participated.

It was almost like, if it was good for the goose than it was good for the gander.

To find the quality people for the laundry, took some time; but gradually got there.

Providers found out how qualified the kept hotel staff really were. Karl and Hans were top-cabin employees. Emily, Sarah and Ursula carried their weight and much more. Erica was absolutely right with keeping those five. They proved they belonged.

In five of the empty rooms on the second floor; they were converted to briefing rooms with tables used for filling out inquiry-forms. We could handle sixty at a time with Emily, Hans and Karl doing the process through presentation and the form completion. The three of them deserve to go up at least one pay-grade.

Asia said, "Karl is just like you are, his mind doesn't stop thinking." "There is far more to him than house-building-security." I agreed.

The company is concentrating on reaching the underemployed workers first. We are finding there are bankers, bakers, cooks, security officers, policemen, truck drivers and many other categories that are recognized as underemployed. Perhaps more categories than what we were expecting.

In our studies, we are finding here in Wiesbaden the number of men and women who do not have driver's licenses. Therefore, we are working with a company who does driver's education to advance the opportunity of employment for those in need.

It is beginning to look that nearly forty-percent of the unemployed in Germany don't have a car and have never driven. This issue is being studied by our group for the best opportunity for those. There are a lot of bus riders in Wiesbaden.

Because of the economic conditions in Germany, there are many companies who have staff missing, but they are going with lower numbers instead of hiring. All due to economics.

Germany has nearly stopped building houses and business buildings, because there are so many available now. This is going to be a long, slow, row to hoe.

Bob Williamson has called an all-staff meeting for ten in the morning. I believe it will become a 'think tank' exercise.

Bob Williamson was at the top of his game. When he said, "well here goes." I knew we were all going to be players. "We have major issues to face." "Our stay here is not going to be easy." "I want your help."

At that time, I knew what was coming; but not how he was going to get there. "Each of you have great thoughts and minds. I want to know what you think. On any topic." "We are in this together, therefore I am asking for your opinion, thoughts, ideas and professional knowledge and what you have learned in the past."

"Our team will review and consider every suggestion. Together, we will make this work and work well. Germany is going through some hard times; we have to be able to help."

"Hopefully, we will start reviewing concepts and ideas within two days. We will review every presentation before any final decisions will be reached and put into place."

"Any questions?" There were none.

I thought about asking Mr. Williamson, but I decided to write like he requested. I was thinking that we needed to talk with Erica about the people who were working in the Hotel's restaurant. We need to keep them employed.

The employees would pay for their own breakfast, lunch and dinner. We would have an entrance into the restaurant from the company lobby; and also, an entrance via the terrace.

For the people who worked nearby our office they could still come to eat breakfast and lunch there. The restaurant would be at least a break-even business.

The second thing I will suggest is to have a committee to decide which categories of work qualities we need to prioritize in getting started.

The staff needs to help Bob and Erica with their overloads.

I believe one of the best suggestions talked about was made by written and made by Asia Lynn. Her statement of "we need to use the expertise of all of our German born employees for they have lived the events, know of the recent financial woes and understand their country. We should use them as the key source of information."

I am going to ask Mr. Williamson if he would like a 'blue line' written on Asia's concept. I want him to know that I support and would help outline the approach that makes the best sense and provides the greater opportunities.

There will be a chapter written about Wiesbaden; the events, activities and success that came there.

CHAPTER TWENTY:
DETERMINING SPAIN

One major decision has been reached about Barcelona, Spain. There are now five who have been selected for the team. They include Blake, Louise, Horatio, Priscilla and Wil Emerson, an accountant in Saint Pete who was the gentleman who laughed at the joke told in Spanish to Horatio.

Wil might have to take a difference job in Spain, but will go to Barcelona because of how strong he is in the Spanish language.

Erica, has been hammering home points as to how important language will become for the future success in Barcelona; that wants most of the Spain employees should be from the group of Latinos who have been working elsewhere for the world.

Anyway, we can break down the language barrier, the better. I don't think there is opposition to her thinking.

At least with the people we can help. Our interviewing process in Barcelona must be perfect in detecting the information we know for sure. And that is not much now

The major question is: what have these people done in the past and simply how many people have no backgrounds or history of work.

Barcelona, as we have learned is not the real Spain as other cities are. But is a city where thousands of people are below the poverty line and we must try to help solve some of their problems.

The best way to learn is to put a dozen Spanish speaking individuals in the locations where the problems are the biggest and try to overcome the issues. Currently, there is not yet a game-plan, but a project is in place to find the game-plan necessary to succeed. Progress is very slow going.

We are not talking about moving a thousand from poverty at a time but perhaps ten or twenty. We have learned for everyone who crawls out of poverty; actually, we get nearly four at a time.

One of the greatest problems here is that the officials in the city and the government doesn't really care if we get any persons out of poverty. The officials don't see the issues as their problem.

Barcelona doesn't have an industry other than tourism which could and will help the less fortunate. On the Med it will be easy to create beach bums; but not practical.

I presented an opinion to Mr. Williamson that we should cut our losses in Spain and work from Germany only.

CHAPTER TWENTY-ONE:
WONDERFUL WIESBADEN

Wiesbaden, Germany is completely different than Barcelona, Spain. Our team is there and in place and most of the study of the German city has been completed. We are using the information from the German members of our team to establish a very reliable factsheet, and common, general knowledge.

I will add some more facts later but this is primarily what we know now of poverty in Wiesbaden. Currently, yesterday's totals indicated that the city was twenty-two-point-two percent under the poverty line. Germany has great reading on people employed; but so many employed are paid under the poverty level.

When the Euros currency began on January 1, 2002; many of the companies were forced to cut back because of the economy. Companies let very few people off but lowered some salaries to maintain staff. Most of the people understood the marketplace and decided not to be let go, but paid a lower salary.

Nearly forty-two percent of the totals under the poverty level are not unemployed, but underemployed. That is a major difference in

Germany than elsewhere. This gives some major news. We have a great number of employed who are proven workers but circumstances have placed them where they are.

It could mean for us to be successful in Wiesbaden would be based on the German economy. We could study this in many different ways, but our initial thinking is that prices have to be lowered until the economy comes back.

There is good material to show where prices are cut, but the volume of sales increases which places the companies in better market position. The problem is however, only a very few companies will follow suit.

We need to study this shortage by knowing what are the professions who were cut back. Completed surveys will answer that question very quickly. What we have to remember is that it makes no sense to train individuals in any field, unless there are companies who are hiring.

As time passes, we continue to learn more. Some information obtained is different than what we expected. The German Government's tax and finance policies are causing growing levels of poverty. What this means is if the government see the influx of income for individuals; then almost immediately the taxes and other program costs are risen. It is a no-win situation.

What was just a German problem for their country has changed a great deal lately, because the open borders which allowed the immigration issue has increased the poverty level because most of the immigrants don't have the backgrounds to work or to be employed.

Advisors to the government point out that twenty-two percent of the population in the country will never rise above the poverty level. This is based on the high rate of people with low incomes.

Because, in the sentences above; people in deep poverty can't and never will take the levels of today any better. Because of the many issues mentioned above, the working people today with lower incomes will never be able to take part in the majority of society's activities.

The question will be asked: why is Providers here? The answer: if Providers can work and increase the level of opportunity of German employed and have their years of service, the experience factor, the people with drive could improve the conditions for some. Some people are far better than no people advancing.

I am knowing that the current situation is not great or beautiful; but I can't walk away from these situations without giving an enormous try and campaign. As long as I think and believe that I can make a difference in the near future; then I am going to fight like hell to help.

Perhaps the area where we can help the most right now is in the urban areas, where poverty is quite high. Mr. Williamson, our top dog, down to the lowest pup we have employed; will engage the enemy and fight on for better conditions.

Mr. Williamson sent a message down stairs to Asia and I to have us come upstairs as soon as possible. We were asked to shut the door. We did. "Please sit down." "This might be a surprise for you both but I don't want you to get started on anything yet in Germany."

"I want the two of you to work on one major project. You will have two weeks to come up with some answers for us. I need you to find us a better location in Europe that would or could be better for us than Barcelona." "The location must be in Europe and not anyplace else."

"The conference room on this floor will be your offices for two weeks." "What are your thoughts?" Asia spoke first. "It will be a challenge but we will do our best." I commented on our budget for the new location, the staffing and the set-up cost projections? "The two of you will determine that."

I looked at Asia Lynn and spoke. The Prime Minister of Spain was right all along.

Asia and I studied cities and communities all through Europe with poverty levels from twelve-percent to over twenty-percent of the people being below the line.

In France, Italy, and through most of Europe we found issues in big cities and even little towns. We keep coming back to the following. Where there is American involvement with military bases or large American corporations in the area; the more the community would like to have assistance from us or the United States.

Our leads keep bringing us back to Germany. This is primarily because we have the involvement with the communities where we have the American military. In these areas the rich are getting richer and the poor are getting more visible and numerous.

The number one choice to replace Barcelona would be Bremerhaven, Germany. There is currently American Naval presence. Currently, there are twenty-two point-seven percent are below the poverty line in Bremerhaven.

Our number two choice would be in Koblenz, Germany. We could work out of the Wiesbaden offices. Koblenz is just up the Reine River. We could advertise in Koblenz as we could in Wiesbaden.

The first message we heard from Mr. Williamson is that we are stopping all potential operations out of Barcelona at this time. It was a mistake in the beginning and now even a bigger mistake.

Our study now is with the twenty-eight people who went to St. Pete for consideration. More later.

The next message from Williamson came about thirty-minutes later. We will have a second location in Germany. Where? The study is being made now. More later.

The twenty-eight who went to St. Pete are being offered a one-year severance: a check for one year of work. We will not go back to the eight countries of the past. We were at a good-place to leave them. The study is ongoing about Germany's number two city. More later.

Mr. Williamson has invited Asia and myself to the office. When we got there, we found Erica and Della there ahead of us. "Thanks for getting here as fast as you did."

"Silas, what is your thinking and what would believe in?" I would like to reconsider my thinking for a moment. If we included Koblenz, it would cost us less and we could do everything from here. That is my first and only choice.

"Asia, your perspective?" "I could argue both sides; being sensible, I would take Koblenz." "Della, tell them what you were thinking." "I wouldn't take on anyone now but Wiesbaden.

This is the city that would give us momentum and success."

"Erica. It is your turn." "I would take the five headed to Barcelona and bring them here. I think Wiesbaden should stand alone." "You all have such creative and thinking minds. Additional thoughts?" Yes, I said. You asked us to find you another city in Europe. If we hadn't got that instruction; I would have said to do Wiesbaden by itself.

I was surprise when Asia stood up. "It is great that you include all of us in your thought process but you must say go or stop. I think it is time for you to say Wiesbaden and we will go for it." Williamson looked out the window and spoke. "It's Wiesbaden by itself. Bring the five from Spain here. We will do some adjusting and we will go from here." I was the first to point out that we have just saved the company a slug of money.

CHAPTER TWENTY-TWO:
DONORS, DOERS, AND DANCERS

I have never seen a company with the quality of leadership, corporate directors and others employed so deep in thought, able to address issues, provide concepts and ideas, and conquer the impossible like this company.

The level of expertise at each level is well above the national standards. The way of approaching a potential employee, the test and exercise they give in the beginning, the interview process, their allowing for a candidate to speak and introduce themselves to the company but also to others who also see employment is courage's.

If the group going to Wiesbaden was a baseball team; this would be my line-up. First up would be Erica House, knows Wiesbaden and all of Germany forward and backward. Number two in the line-up is Della Sharp. His last name says it all. In the third position is Asia Dash. She knows it before you finish teaching it.

In the clean-up position as number four is Bob Williamson. We all work for him. He is dynamite. Number five is Silas Fox. He stirs the coals and a flash of ideas come to his mind. Number six is Jason O'Dea; his mind is a like a steel-trap. Sharp.

Number seven is the watchdog: Katarina Damaris. She will keep us safe. In the eighth position is Jill St. Cloud. She is the back-half of salt and pepper. Another former FBI agent on our team. And number nine is Ursula Wagner. Qualified to do almost anything. And we have a bench strength that is out of this world.

This is a team of brains, talent, and devotion to completion and complete detail throughout. Williamson is the manager, any or all at some time or another will be considered coach, or team leader. This group is ready and capable.

CHAPTER TWENTY-THREE:
WALTZING IN WIESBADEN IS NOT AS EASY AS THE TWO-STEP

We will offer hope in Wiesbaden with sessions in English, French, German and Spanish. Horatio and Pricilla are saved.

Blake Tate will become a German watchdog becoming an overseer of scheduling for those being invited to attend. Louise will continue to take pictures and build a history of development through photography.

Wil Emerson, will be assigned to work with the German gentlemen down stairs. He is so sharp he will be speaking German within a few weeks.

Mr. Williamson will get to work within the couple of days with all of us following the need and concept.

The advertising concept in Wiesbaden has worked tremendously. From the first thousand forms which were filled out by those attending our sessions have given us great information.

A little over eighty-percent of the people have worked before. Of those eighty-percent of the people, a total now of forty-seven percent are employed but are underemployed.

Once we got the information on the people there were twenty-seven companies, we approached asking on behalf of the people a four-percent increase in their wages. Nineteen of those companies gave the raises.

Our immediate concern following the form's information was about fifteen-percent of the people were living above their means in housing that they couldn't afford and should never had rented.

It was tough to explain to the people involved but basically it worked like this. For example. Instead of paying rent of eight-hundred-dollars and dropping to five-hundred-dollars gave the people a three-hundred dollar a month raise to be used for other expenses. You would be completely surprised to know that twenty-three percent of the people filling out are questionnaire fell into that category.

For those that moved to a lower cost location on the average was gaining for their selves; more than two-hundred-dollars per month savings. It did not take the people out of poverty but gave them considerably more money for other expenses.

We found out also that smaller communities around the city had similar job opening and lacked the people with skills to fill them. Again, more salary, lower cost for apartment, and more available money per month to use.

We ended up in that first thousands of having some type of activity; we increased the income levels for people without taking them out of the poverty level they were in. But gave an opportunity to advance their life's capability.

In several cases we were able to convince the wife to stop working and living on the husband's income. The travel costs for the wife and the cost of paying for child care was more of an issue than what they had not realized.

Even with one position eliminated, the family's status improved with the change. Some people can see the forest because of the trees. In the first group of people, we had data sheets on we increased their position but without taking them out of under the poverty line.

By asking the employer for additional funding and adjusting the start and quitting times each day; one-hundred-eighteen people were now just over the poverty line and they all felt good about themselves. Providers did nothing but asked the employer to reconsider salary levels of individuals.

The company is now doing the information from the second thousand forms and will soon be attacking those.

In addition of what I told you of those above; we also found eighty-jobs for those who were unemployed. Are they out of the poverty line? No, but they are working.

One thing that I must tell you involved an incident involving Mr. Williamson. Bob Williamson walked into a Deutsch bank to open a Providers account in Germany. He walked into bank and walked directly into a bank robbery and was taken hostage immediately. Katarina was across the street with a great view of the front door. Jill St. Cloud was walking around in front of the bank until he came out again.

In a short period of time the robber holding a gun in his right hand and hanging on to Bob walked out of the bank and was standing in front of the door. It was Katarina across the street who fired a perfect shot and the gun was on the sidewalk.

Jill knocked the robber to the ground, stood on his hand that had been shot, pulled her gun and placed the head of the pistol into the robber's mouth. He started to move and she cocked the weapon. He didn't move again.

The Wiesbaden police officer took charge, Jill packing all of the jack; showed the officer her credentials. By then Katarina came across the street and told Jill that she owed her a bullet. Mr. Williamson was gaining control again, spoke; "I'll buy you each a bullet." He said then, "Let's get back to the office."

I was told, the three walked down the street with Mr. Williamson having both arms around the shoulders of the former FBI agents. Just another day in Germany.

Reference the second round of a thousand forms. Again, we used the same formula with some favorable results. We placed unemployed to work but not the same number as the first and we reached some more companies to raise the salaries by four percent. People not out of poverty; but far better off than before.

Our system is working and another batch of forms to go through. I am sorry to say that there is about ten-percent of the applicants that are not employable.

CHAPTER TWENTY-FOUR:
BEING OVER THEN BEGINING AGAIN

Asia and I have had over forty-months of brain-testing, spending of energy, travel, multiple times to Europe, back again and around the Continent trying to aid the cause in helping Providers become what they now are in Europe.

On the anniversary of our three-year date with the company; our discussions led us to believe that it was time to get off this merry-go-round and head back to the quiets of the Northwest.

We were not talking Seattle, Bremerton of anything too big; our minds and hearts were building our home in Seabeck and also to have a yacht docked on the water-front of the Hood's Cannel.

The house was going to big enough for us to have visitors, for Asia to have a designing studio with everything she needs and for me to have an office where I can call on my journalism past and write accounts of our travels.

We also wanted to have a little Chapel like room in the house where anyone who visits or us staying there could talk to 'The Father' whenever the time came to do so.

When we arrived back in Florida and visited to say our good-byes in St. Pete; we laughed, cried, joked, were serious, told stories, lies, and tried to remain cool because we both wanted to head to the Northwest.

Asia called and talked to her-daughter Cindy for some time, but didn't set a date to visit. I called my dad and said we are flying through Chicago and headed to Spokane to drive down and see you for a couple of days.

I asked my dad if he could have my car serviced before we got there. He told me tomorrow. The airport in Chicago was the typical airport in Chicago that we all hate, the arrival in Spokane was quiet, and the one-way-rent to Moscow was easy to pull off.

My parent's home was so fresh and nice, it was ready for a major magazine to take pictures. It ended up that it was me taking the pictures. When the time came, we both felt relaxed and that we were ready to move on.

The weather was perfect all the way to Seabeck. The only room available at the Best Western on the water front was a small suite with two king-sized beds. No problems for the two of us; two lovers to be in the near future. The six-years were up.

It was during the early evening on that March date of 2004 that Asia told me it had been long enough and since she had talked to her daughter and had told her daughter what she was going to do; it was time to do it.

Asia asks me to marry her. I accepted but said there is something I had to do. I found my appropriate piece of luggage and recovered a very small box that I had been hiding since Wiesbaden. You all know what is in the box.

I asked Asia if she would wear my diamond-ring I purchased in Germany for this very special occasion. She was thrilled. I was too, but I stayed in my own bed that evening. The next day we traveled from Seabeck to Port Orchard to the Kitsap County Court House and got our marriage license.

There were six more nights sleeping alone. The wedding at the little Chapel in Lonerock was unable to book us until then. The reception will be at the Conference Grounds.

A major topic of discussion during those days waiting, was the topic of the design of Asia's clothing line. The primary question was what to call the women's line plus what also to call the men's line.

She asked me to put in my two-cent's worth and I did have some thoughts of both. My thought for a women's line was: The Finest by Asia Fox. On the men's line: The Sly Fox by Asia.

I didn't know if I needed to go any further. I did move forward. I could vision a very small outline of a fighter-jet with after-burners-red-hot. It would honor the memory of her first husband and Cindy's dad.

My thoughts were to promote the men's line with a percentage of profit going to the Wounded Warriors or some military organizations helping spouses and family members financially.

I knew living in Seabeck, she didn't have to carry stacks of designs to the East Coast but only to Seattle. The Nordstroms Department Stores headquarters was in the Emerald City. They produced their own lines for both Nordstroms and the Nordstroms' Rack outlets.

Another reason I mentioned staying in Seattle was the Pacific Northwest was one of the Mecca for military bases in the Country: The Whidbey Naval Air Station in Seattle, the Puget Sound Navy Ship Yard in Bremerton, Bangor Submarine Base in Bangor, the McChord Air Force Base in Tacoma, and Fort Lewis, just south of Tacoma.

The Pacific Northwest loves the military. I can't forget across the State near Spokane was the SAC Base, Fairchild Air Force Base. I could picture clothes for both men and women in the primary colors of the military uniforms. Navy blue, Air

Force blue, and Army green. The military fighter-jet insignia would fly-high in the Northwest.

Best of all, the brand's promotion could feature Asia as a retired Air Force Lieutenant Colonel now doing designing which she loves and she hasn't forgotten about his service record and that her first husband was an AF fighter-pilot killed in a jet-plane crash.

Asia cried real alligator tears when I told her and showed her my concept. I think it was the hardest she ever hugged me, Result, she wasn't necessarily pleased with the concept for the name on the women's line; but loved the idea of trying the Seattle market-place. Like me, she still loved the military.

I listened very closely when she spoke. "Thank you. I think that I will have a professional-presentation available six to nine months from now." "I am honored that you thought of my first husband in your concept." "You are the only man in my life now, but from times back them. Something's still linger."

When I think of what my dad said years ago, there are things in his mind that still linger from the days with my mother. And I appreciate that for both my dad and Asia, their past will sometimes speak to them. Both of them will have new spouses.

Changing the subject, Asia asked. "Is the order still the house, business-your book and then boat?" I told her; I think so. She added. "Can we go fishing?" Later. "Yes, I know; when the tide comes in."

If you think the story is over; think again. It is not.

Asia has been very successful with her new line of clothes. It took her about nine months to get to see the people of importance at Nordstrom's in Seattle. They loved and accepted about eighty-percent of her line of clothes designed for Nordy's and the Rack.

During the same time period I was successful and completed the writing and published my first book: OFF THE CUFF. It hasn't gone over as well as I wanted it to, but it is out there and I have a show-and-tell piece with my name on it.

I have been working on my second book, research has taken a long-time to nearly complete the manuscript. I had to do something to spend my time on and try to stop the hurting that has gone within me for the last two-plus-years since Asia's accident.

It was right after the first of the year in 2006 when on a winter's day In January that a logging truck lost control of the rig and the truck hit Asia's car on her way to the Silverdale Mall for a design showing of a new winter line.

She did not die at the scene of the accident, but three-days later at the Harrison Memorial Hospital in Bremerton. She is buried at the Forest Lawn Cemetery in Bremerton.

Her death brought many people from Providers to the funeral. Thankfully, the Kitsap County Sun, did an outstanding article on Asia when she died. The article included information about how her first husband the pilot, died as well.

Today, nearly two and one-half years later; I am still in Seabeck and I am sitting at a small table in the General Store having a roast-beef sandwich. No fries, only a drink: Doctor Pepper.

I don't look like a Marine anymore; my hair is much longer and my horn-rimmed glasses have changed my appearance somewhat. I still love the outdoors and spend a lot of time on my boat: Asia's Dream.

The walking of the docks is still a daily ritual for me and probably will be.

CHAPTER TWENTY-FIVE:
GUESS WHO SHOWED UP

I was just finishing my sandwich when a woman wearing dark-glasses and a scarf over her head walked up to my table. She asked, "Are you Silas Franklyn Fox?" Yes, I am.

"Hello, I am Asia's friend from the Air Force years ago; my name is Grace." Please be seated. Can I buy you lunch or a beverage? "Just a tall, big bottle of water would be great."

With the water our conversation began. "The rat-race and the nasty groups of people in my profession got old and upsetting. Most were too liberal for me." "Several years ago, Asia invited me to Seabeck to visit." I remember that. "Well, I am finally here?" I am glad you are.

"I asked the young-man working in the front of the store if the man sitting in the back was you. Yep, was his answer. Now, here I am." I asked, so what are your plans. "Right now, I don't have any; I just want to cool my heels." You have come to the right place.

"Asia said years ago that Seabeck was gorgeous and a great place to relax. So, I thought I would see for myself." Have you seen any of it so far? "No, I just got here. I need to rent a hotel room and get comfortable."

If you don't think this is too forward; I have a large house and plenty of bedrooms and I would love to take you boating and seeing the sites on Puget Sound. "I think I would love that. Can we start by walking the dock?"

Sure, do you like to fish? "I don't know, I never have." Maybe we can try this evening. That would be; later when the tide comes in.

"I want to tell you something that Asia Lynn told me in one of our conversations. She said sometimes, you are too much a gentleman." "That's something that I thought you should know. Please keep that in mind."

Thank you for sharing that news. Me, being a gentleman is caused by both Asia and you both being such beautiful and wonderful women. I think that sometimes you have to wash and polish the car; before you get to drive it.

What's next? "When do they stop serving lunch?" She was hungry.

When I look back and think of Asia and then look now at Grace; Asia was correct in the fact they are both very much alike in looks. However, I believe the persona and personality of Grace is considerable different. Time will tell.

One thought to ponder. I don't think that Grace came to Seabeck to fish and look at the water. There was a bigger fish to fry. Time will tell. Ops I just said that.

I told Grace there was a full-walk out apartment on the bottom floor of our house. Someday perhaps it is going to be used by my parents. Now it is empty of people, but fully furnished. There is a way to get into the main house from the apartment without going outside.

"I would like to see it and I would like to know what the rent amount would be?" Well, since it is you; I will rent it to you for one-dollar-per-month. There must be some type of a charge.

When I told her she could use the design studio at no charge; she almost cried. She spoke. "Not only are you too much a gentleman, you are way too nice." "If you are serious about this, I will take it and be honored to be here."

To tell you the truth, I was happier than Grace was. I always try to match a name to what the name's meaning is. The meaning of the name Grace is favor and blessings.

This Grace, now in Seabeck, understands humanity, charity, kindness, and I believe cooperation. She is comfortable being in the house and I am pleased that she is in the house, contented and who knows what will develop.

I am glad that she speaks from the heart and doesn't beat around the bush like Asia did. With this, I believe that we are strengthen by her being here. She is not a put on and her life's skilled have allowed her to be successful for all that she has done.

Her questions don't come from a harsh voice but from a soft voice who truly wants an answer to the question which was asked. I told Grace directly that Asia had said years ago that you were an outstanding designer. But you lacked time, space and needed equipment. What is in the studio it is yours to use?

Grace has a developed, athletic body, but doesn't try to flaunt it. She is what she is from the inside out. There is no mistake about who she is, but I believe in her thinking she is more mature in her daily life than Asia was and has a heart of gold; once said by Asia.

Grace was sorry that Seabeck didn't have a bowling alley. She carried about a one-sixty-average in the last league she was in. I asked her about her military time in the service to the country. She said she liked her work; could easily take orders and direction but also didn't mind giving orders and direction to those below her in rank. She said she tried to help everyone and still get her work done and more.

"Tell me about you boat 'Asia's Dream?" It is an inboard-Chris Craft, twenty-four-feet long and it sleeps four. It is easy to fish from and it is beautiful on the inside. On the very back it has SEABECK WASHINGTON as its home of record.

"I believe the desert we purchased earlier today and a cup of Folger's coffee should be made by the person with less fish. I believe that if we each have the same number of fish; we should do what it says in the Bible." What is that? "Hebrews." That's fine with me.

The float on the Sound was perfect. The sunset was colorful and the company was very pleasant. The fish were not biting and both of us didn't care. "Tomorrow we will catch some and the bet will remain the same." Okay, I get to choose the desert tomorrow night.

"Anything but hot apple pie." How about one of Silas's ice cream Sunday's? "Yum." The rest of the evening past without anything exciting happening.

In the morning the first time I saw her, I asked 'when do you want your next boat ride?' "I will go grab my sweater." I need about an hour to finish what I had started this morning. On the way out, let's stop at the General Store for a roast beef sandwich. Is that good with you? "Certainly."

Grace, is a breath of fresh air. She has turned out to be exactly who she said she was; honest and direct. I finished my work doing the balancing of the check-book and I told her I was ready to go.

She was there in a flash. I didn't wait until she finished her make-up or her hair. It seems to me she is very well organized. I asked her if she wanted to attend Chapel with me this week? Her response was special. "I would love to, if you think the people would accept me after all of the time that you and Asia attended."

I told Grace that I wouldn't care if they were harsh; you and I are together and they must accept us as a couple. We have certainly reached the level of girlfriend and boyfriend, and certainly growing closer to each other day by day.

We have had our sandwich and have taken the boat out into the channel. I asked Grace if she would like to be the driver for a while and become the skipper of the Asia's Dream? She couldn't believe the offer. But said yes.

Grace, doesn't have to be given lessens; she has been watching, learning and understanding the duties and responsibilities of the skipper. She asked. "Was I comfortable for a few minutes being the first-mate? I told her, that I would probably be comfortable for a life-time. She said, "I would love that."

We found a place to anchor the boat off channel so we could fish. I landed the first silver, a beautiful fish; perhaps ten-pounds. I said nothing about it until Grace went ahead of me three fish to one.

I reported to her that I had lost and I again would prepare coffee and treats. I then took the time to explain what will soon happen when Puget Sound changes from smooth water to chopping water in a short period of time.

I will lift the anchor and start the engine and turn us around facing toward home. I expect rain within the hour and I think we better cover the back with the tarps before we leave. That was done and we were finally ready.

She came up close to me and we both stood nearby the wheel. We didn't make Seabeck before the rains kept coming, coming harder, and coming where the vision out of the window was difficult to see. That evening the Lord guided this twenty-four-footer to its safe and secure docking place.

We got good and wet while tying down and getting to the car. Once in the car, she grabbed my hand and said thank you. She was wet and looked worn out; but was beautiful to see.

She later came upstairs in the house and we drank dark hot coffee, looked out of the window at the rain and storm and listened to easy going music on my system. She asked me "do you want to dance?" Not tonight I said, you are far too electric. But very soon I told her.

I knew we were both falling in love. It happens to millions every day. But I still believe you shouldn't rush into things.

I won't tell you about the next six-month; day to day activities we both did. I will only mention that I finished my second book and she was nearly completed with another set of beautiful designs. The past six month gave me enough time to prepare for the future.

I walked down the hallway and stopped at the design office door. I knocked. "Come in please." "Is there something I need to do?" Yes, I would like you to come with me for a drive to Silverdale. "Why." She spoke.

I want to go to a jeweler and pick out and buy your engagement ring and our rings of marriage; if you will marry me? Grace, I love you and will you be my wife? "Yes, yes. Yes." I grabbed her like never before.

The white-gold rings were selected, sized and prepared for delivery. I paid the mega bucks and I truly didn't care. The engagement ring was on her left hand and slowly we made our way back to Seabeck.

Grace Anne Story has a story that needs to be told. When she was very young, her best friend was the reflection in the mirror. As an only and lonely child with strict parents her time to be adventurist was limited. That was one of the great reasons why she learned to be a great student.

Her life changed quickly when her dad died when she was in the sixth grade. Her mother was loving and allowed far more time for her to grow and blossom. She in high school, was the cheerleading captain, the homecoming queen and graduated in the top ten in her class. She had several scholarships.

Her great looks created the opportunity in cheerleading and homecoming court; her initial study habits allowed for academic success. Even so, with all of the achievements she was somewhat a loner. Didn't date much and was always thinking about her future career.

She was even then a beautiful untouchable. At the University of Omaha, she tried to stay hidden, but achieved academic stardom. She was top in her class of the School of Finance and finished second in her class of Business Development. Grace was on the President's list of achievement and finished college with a grade-point-average of three-point-nine-three.

I might point out she was asked multiple time to be photographed for magazine covers and she turned all of them down. Today, she is in her realm. Soon to be the bride of Silas Fox; she is gracious, happy and she too is living a dream. Grace Story is far more than what can be said about her. She wins the award for being America's most wonderful.

Silas asked today. Grace, lets pack an overnight bag in case we don't get back and let's cruise the Sound on a much longer trip. We will pass Silverdale, Poulsbo, Bainbridge Island, see Bremerton, Port Orchard, Annapolis, Waterman and then head home. The boat is prepared for an overnighter.

By the time we got to Bainbridge Island; it was time to find cove to hunker-down in. Not far from shore, but far out enough on Puget Sound. She was quiet for a while and finally she spoke. "John Denver sang that West Virginia was almost heaven. He was wrong; this is heaven on earth, here, right now." I didn't disagree.

The morning sun was bright, no clouds and only a fine chop on the water. We had sweet rolls and juice for breakfast. The next part of the trip was to head to Bremerton and to float by the Great War Ships in drydock. We would then cross the inlet to view Port Orchard from the water and then go further to Annapolis and farther down the water front to Waterman.

In that water we would look out for other private boats, ferries, boats of the Navy, a few sail boats and maybe a dingy or two.

She picked up a copy of my new book: THE FANCY FOX. "Why that title she asked?" Because men can see beauty too. In paintings, in the arts, music, theater, operas and many more things. When Asia was killed, I needed to find classics in every category you could think of to help stop the pain of her loss.

Grace, the world is beautiful if you slow down and enjoy it. I don't hustle anymore; I look for kindness, care and freedoms. It is special to see a rainbow, a sunset, a full moon. Years ago, I booked everywhere I went. Now, I like to write them, read them, review them and purchase from beginning writers.

In my partner, I see respect, purpose, gentleness, love and mostly understanding. That is, you to a tee. Let's go home.

I have two bad knees but Grace has filled out my dance card. There is an old saying that I love that would work for us. "If you will dance with me in the rain, you will walk with me through a storm." Those days are coming.

When we got back to the house there were phone messages from dad and Jasper. I called my dad and he said that he and Brenda are about ninety-days out. I reminded him there were two yachts for sale in Shelton; but both would cost him some money.

When I got a hold of Jasper, he told me I could get an early out; then go through with retirement in about thirty days. He gave me information on property, house, small airplane hangar, and plenty of space. He asked if I could go do a look and see about the place. I told him yes.

A couple of days ago, Grace went and viewed the arrangement at the Willows in East Bremerton for her mother. She loved the place and thought it was well worth the monthly cost. She got in touch with her mother and then called the Willows that her mother would take a one-bedroom unit.

Grace's mother loves to do lots of fun things including working with clay and ceramics. She has taken up the hobby of painting, continues to sew and loves to embroider.

The Willows also provides transportation to stores like Hobby Lobby where she could and would pick up product for her using. There is also a Michael's store with more choice and opportunity.

When she is at the Willows she could certainly come and visit and we could and would go to her too. One other thing that her mother says about the Willows is they have great food and provide three great meals a day plus snacks.

Grace's mother would bring much of her favorite belonging with her. The Willows is a very popular place and she is lucky that she could get right in. Ms. Angus Story will be in Kitsap County in just under a month from now. Grace will help with the move in and the set up for her mother.

I went to look at the property for Jasper and found it to be suited for what he needed. But I added that I thought the asking price was about thirty-grand too high. Without telling Jasper, I also went and saw a place closer to Seabeck that I thought would work better. The price was also better.

I called Jasper and told him of my discovery. He asked if it could be a pricing war between the two places? No, you don't want to go there. The Seabeck cost and location is that much better. It is closer to the farms and ranches just north of here.

Jasper has been a very successful rancher and has plans to sell the animals and the house. The leads to what he wants to establish here locally. From Seabeck going towards Holly there are several small ranches and farms that could use farming equipment from time to time.

Near Cheyenne he currently has tractors, and all earth working equipment for planting, cutting, storage and shipping products and animals. That the part of the belonging he would bring to set up a working co-op locally.

Grace came forward and told me her thoughts for the wedding. I want a late afternoon wedding on the Conference Grounds and invite the citizens of Seabeck to come and celebrate with us. "These are our neighbors and they should be included."

I would like to wear a white pants suit with a colorful blouse. You could wear a comfortable summer suit. I would like to call a caterer and tell him or her that we would like to spend a thousand dollars and for him or her to provide the meat and cake.

In the invitation for the Seabeck crowd, we will introduce the wedding and invite them to bring a favorite dish for a pot-luck. The wedding celebrating and reception would begin at four-o'clock in the afternoon. This would be four-weeks from this Saturday.

I would like to have the Pastor and his wife who do the wedding programs at the Conference Grounds to be the one who officiates. I would be happy to make visitations and phone calls with you to get this done. We could advertise the wedding and the invitation to the people of Seabeck in hand out at stores and shops in the area.

Absolutely no wedding gifts. Them bringing a favorite item for the pot-luck is certainly enough from each. Come and get to know us better and let us get to know you. I told her I was ready.

The Conference Ground said yes. The Pastor and his wife; Dr. Jason and Kimberly Peters also said yes. When we called the first catered, she said she couldn't do it by herself. But she knew two others that could help. She would be back to us.

The answer came back to us later the same day and she said yes. The three with primary food responsibilities said we would like to do a Texas barbeque. They would provide the carvers, paper plates, silverware and all others needed.

I called my dad and asked if he would like to stand up for me. He said he would but he thought I should invite someone from Seabeck that everyone knows, and I said, like the Pastor of the Lonerock Church and Chapel. "Exactly."

Pastor Taylor said he would love to be the best man. Grace said I know who I would like to ask: Janet, Jasper's wife. I told Grace that we have never met her yet. Grace answered, "So." Janet, was surprise but honored and said yes.

We called a bottling company in Bremerton and they said yes; they would provide large ice containers and ice down enough soft drinks for the crowd for the afternoon. They thought it would cost about six hundred dollars.

I stood in line at the General Store buying a loaf of whole-wheat bread when a very tall, distinguished looking gentlemen introduced himself to me. Dr. Sean T. Kelly, a D.O. with a Master's Degree in Public Health. Formerly of Colorado Springs. "I had heard of Seabeck before and I found out that the community needed another doctor, that was my clue to come."

Doctor Kelly, who stands about six-foot five-inches-tall; must have had some hoops in him earlier. He said, "my wife and I are looking for a home on the water-front and we are good for about a half-a-million. Do you know of any homes?"

There are about four or five that I know. I would go check with 'Stand the man reality,' about two city blocks down the road on the right side of the street.

Dr. Kelly, my name if Silas Fox; I am a beginning writer on my third book after years in the military and professional business. I welcome you to Seabeck.

By the way I am getting married and the community of Seabeck has been invited to our wedding on the Conference Grounds in about three weeks. I would love to have you and your wife attend. "I will note my calendar."

We both got back in line again. I am looking for someone to do drawings for details in my new manuscript. Doctor Kelly said. "You should talk to my wife; she has been a professional artist for years."

I don't know if I could afford her services? "I think if you would take me salmon fishing, I think we could work something out." I gave Sean my telephone number. It is Colorado Springs's lost. Seabeck wins again.

Our conversation didn't stop there. Sean said, "I do make house calls." "Especially if a call is on the dock next to a yacht." We could fish later today if you wanted to after the tide comes in. "I don't have the equipment." I got you covered.

Let's take our women too. They would get a chance to know each other. I gave Sean all of the information and directions to the boat. Five o'clock is the time. When I got home to tell Grace, she was ready to go then.

Grace and Lois talked liked they have been friends for years. Sean and I each caught fish. The sunset was beautiful and the fishing and the boat ride was beyond expectations.

Grace and Lois are in the house and in the design studio. I guess the boat ride was enough to make Grace feel comfortable with Lois seeing the designs she is currently finishing for the next show in Seattle.

It was my understanding, according to Grace that by seeing the designs she might have an idea as to how the display boards could be jazzier and up-beat. Time will tell.

CHAPTER TWENTY-SIX:
THE SETTLERS IN SEABECK

Let me point out that the book; LATER WHEN THE TIDE COMES IN is far from over. So many more stories to tell, information on the people moving to the Seabeck community, the up-coming marriage and much more. We will make room for you if you want to come.

We are looking for a boat docking location where the Asia's Dream can go into a slip that is covered. The location has to be close to us.

Grace has some things in storage that needs to be shipped to us for our lives to be better blended. Our house is going to be made over with furnishings changes. No renovations planned at this time.

The down stairs furniture has to be removed because dad and Brenda will be bringing their own belongings, plenty of books and desks for both of them to be using while writing their books.

My dad has asked if I would do some advance search for a small yacht for the two of them to enjoy the waters of Puget Sound. I think he wants to name is boat the "Idahoan". He loves the state but he loves his family more.

My parents would like a new cabin-over yacht that sleeps six to eight and is primarily set up to spend time on the water for pleasure. They both have photography hobbies and could put one-hundred-thousand into the craft. There are a couple of yachts to look at in Shelton that might be the ticket.

Grace has a concept for additional designs, dad and Brenda want to start writing their books; and I am looking to start my third one myself: IT'S OVER WHEN IT IS OVER.

I am thinking that Jasper and Janet could use some of the furniture what is here.

I talked with Sean Kelly's wife Lois and she shown an interest in what I was doing. So told me how far along I need to be before she could step in and provide her service.

Naturally, I had to pursue her name a little further. On her business card was the name Lois Lane Kelly. This Lois was lovely and talented compared with the Lois Lane at the Daily Planet of Superman.

What I found out that our Seabeck Lois has a full name of Lois Elizabeth Lane Kelly. In grade school and in high school she was called Liz. In college Elizabeth was used. In professional life she became Lois Lane Kelly.

This is what she suggested to do. I wanted to use about twelve pictures in my book. She thought I should use the pictures and she would do a pen and ink drawing on the same picture on opposite pages. I thought it was a great idea.

She also said that she has plans to do a children's book with a similar concept.

She also said that her husband Sean had a great photographic eye and his work; a hobby, was outstanding.

I don't want to tell you what my new book is about until you finish reading this one. I will tell you one thing. The book covers many concepts or issues one by one with the outlook it will be over when it is over.

Seabeck is becoming an artist location with painters, writers, designers, and graphic illustrators. We should form a corporation under one set of by-laws and by public and personal presentation. When one gets seen, all get seen at the same time.

The Corporation – the Seabeck Settlers Group was formed three weeks later. Let me give you the concept as to whom it will benefit: Dad, Brenda, Lois, Grace, Sean, Jasper, Janet and myself.

Lastly, we are having a blast. When one is recognized, all eight will be given recognition. Recognition will be given to books, designs, and the elegance of Seabeck. Nothing is more beautiful than the water and the surrounding areas.

I got a call and I couldn't believe it. Horatio and Priscilla are only two lefts in the house. The younger two are in college and the other two are on their own. Horatio asked. "Is there room for two more in Seabeck?" He told me that he knows the Puget Sound region and he loved it when he was there in the Navy years ago.

I asked him what he would be looking for in Seabeck. He spoke, "both a house and a boat. Probably a twenty- or twenty-four-footer. But no submarines.

Okay, what about a house? "A little under a half-million."

I said to myself all we need now are Della and Jason and Savannah and Alan. I don't think S and A are leaving Texas.

It is a week out before the wedding, I have received calls from the Kiwanis, the VFW, and the Conference Ground committee for volunteering for the set up on the wedding day. Tables, chairs, sound systems, and umbrellas to provide shade.

As I told you before Seabeck, Washington is different then what you find most places. Seabeck has always been a community of people, who volunteer and ask how can we help? This will happen at nine am and will go on for as long as it takes. Tear down will be the same way.

Someone asked me the other day where were Grace and I going on our honeymoon. I asked back. Why would you go someplace when you are already living in one of the greatest communities in the world? We are staying home.

I looked at my messages and discovered that the Williamson will be coming to the wedding. They are already back from Europe. He and Mr. Carlson have sold the business and he is now a free man.

I also studied and found that Sean Kelly is a graduate of Rocky Vista University, College of Osteopathic Medicine with a specialty in orthopedics. His Master Degree in Public Health is a feather in his cap for sure. Best of all, he is a great guy and fits into Seabeck as if he was raised here.

I now can understand our wedding is going to be a quiet affair with about four-hundred residents, two dozen close friends, two former FBI agents, an All-American football player, a man who might run for Congress in Florida and a network of people who respect and love each other's.

The information I got from KIRO Radio in Seattle and also KBRO in Bremerton said the day will be bright and sunny.

When I was talking with Doctor Peters, we spoke of this isn't your normal rodeo. His wife Kimberly will lead the gathering with a Christian song most in the crowd will be able to sing by memory. It is during the song that I and my best-man will appear on the platform which the ceremony will be done on.

Paster Peters, said the ceremony will be short, long enough to get you officially hitched. I was glad to hear that. Grace will come up the aisle half-way by herself and that is where I will go to meet her and we will walk the rest of the way forward. The ceremony is not going to be rehearsed.

Dad and Mom along with Graces' mom will be here tomorrow. They will all be staying in bedrooms in the big-house. We have booked seven room at the Best Western almost to Lonerock.

A lot of people like Jasper and Janet will be doing a wide variety of things while they are her. One of which is to look at the furniture in the down-stairs apartment and to see if they would like any of it. What they want will be free. He just has to buy one bottle of Baileys.

Grace and I will probably see each other on the day of the wedding before the ceremony. Lois, Janet, Katarina, Jill, and others will pretend to help Grace. I will have my body guards too; but they won't be packing jack. If you are wondering what 'jack' is; it means you have multiple weapons on your body.

This is a point of interest for the community. Yesterday, I had a phone call from one of Seabeck's oldest residents, Cheryl Orchards. She asked that during the reception if she could address the crowd and announce something that would be big for the community. Sure, I said.

Out of respect, following the official part of the wedding; she will be called on to speak first. I found out that Ms. Orchards was an elementary school teacher here in the community for years. He late husband was a former oil company executive for Texaco.

I am going to ask Bob Williamson to act as the master of ceremonies. There will be several people flying in that I know will have something to say. Hopefully some of which will be good.

CHAPTER TWENTY-SEVEN: *WEDDING DAY*

I couldn't believe my eyes for the number of men, young and old; and the pick-up trucks which arrived for set up. A Conference Ground director was there and was prepared. He quickly organized the guys and they were moving.

He asked me if there was anything I needed for sure? I answered just to make sure there was two microphone set-ups on the stage. He asked anything else? I said, I don't believe so. He then said that I will see you at three and it was time for me to leave.

Before I left the grounds, I went by the three barbeque pits in the ground to see about four hundred pounds of beef beginning to cook. The fires have been burning for hours. I tasted the sauces from the three areas and they made me hungry. Outstanding.

Just before I crossed the bridge; I could see when they were planning to park about two hundred cars. I said to myself; who is going to pay for all of this? I knew that answer.

I went back to the house and I found a group of guys sitting outside so I joined them.

Williamson asked. "Are you nervous?" I answered should I be? About eight of the other guys all answered together. "Yes."

About eleven o'clock, about ten of us went to the Country Store to have lunch. To our surprised; eleven women including Grace were there having lunch themselves. She smiled and blew me a kiss.

Politely, we waited until the girls were done before we went back in to order. I reminded the guys that I had seen this morning about four hundred pounds of beef being readied for a BBQ. Most of us had tuna fish for our meal.

Several of us walked the dock and I showed them the yacht. They were impressed. Mr. Williamson joked when he asked. "I paid you that much money?" There was some laughter.

It was two and it was time to head back to the house and get dressed for the wedding.

When I got back to the Conference Grounds it was twenty-minutes to four. There were probably one-hundred cars already parked in the lot. I ran into Pastor Taylor and we journeyed to out assigned spots. We would walk up to the stage when Kimberly Peters was preparing to lead the music.

At four-o'clock Ms. Peters walked up to the microphone asked the people to settle in for a wonderful late Saturday afternoon of a wedding, and a joyful celebration.

She told a story about a little church in the Vale and made it sound like the little Chapel at Lonerock. She asked the crowd to join her in singing: The Church in the Wildwood. "There is a Church in the Vale by the Wildwood – no lovelier spot in the Dale." There were probably a hundred and fifty people singing with her as many late comers were crossing the bridge getting to the chairs.

"No place is so dear in my childhood – as the little brown Church in the Dale."

It was time for Pastor Taylor and I to walk up to the stage.

"Come to the Church in the Wildwood, oh come to the Church in the Vale – No spot is so clear in my childhood as the little brown Church in the Vale."

Ms. Peters asked to the crowd to rise as Grace was seen in the back of the chairs down the aisle. Grace started her slow walk up the aisle as the group rose and sang. "How sweet on a Sunday morning to listen to the clear ringing bell. Its tones so sweet are callings – oh, come to the Church in the Vale."

When I saw Grace starting to walk up to aisle was my queue to walk down and meet her. She reached for my arm the moment the music stopped. It was like we had rehearsed the gathering.

When we walked toward the stage Janet and Pastor Taylor stepped to their places. We both made the climb up the four steps very easily. The flowers Grace was carrying were handed to Janet.

Dr. Peters looked at the two of us wearing a big smile. "So, I guess this is it." We smiled back. Doctor Peters looked at me and asked "Why are we here today, Silas?" My answer was to full-filling a dream of my life-time. "Grace, same question to you." "I am going to be married to the man I love."

Doctor Peters and the assembled guests heard each of us say our vows and he continued with the service. Doctor Peters said, "There is not one person here that opposes your marriage; so, let's get on with it."

He asked the usual questions to both of us. "Do you take Grace to be your wife until death do you part?" I do. The question for Grace, "do you take Silas to be your husband until death do you part?" "I do."

Doctor Peters went on. "In this wonderful community of Seabeck, in the fabulous Kitsap County, in the great State of Washington, I now declare you legally married." "You may kiss the bride." So, I did.

We were then introduced as Mr. and Mrs. Silas Fox. The crowd applauded. We remained on stage, center stage in two comfortable chairs.

At the other microphone on the other edge of the stage; Bob Williamson began to speak.

He said, "My name is Bob Williamson, I get the pleasure of introducing a series of speakers for a variety of reasons. I would like to have Mrs. Cheryl Orchards come forward." She was helped onto the stage.

She centered herself at the microphone and leaned on her cane. She began. "I want to thank Silas and his bride for the opportunity of speaking this evening." "My remarks will be short in time but as important as could be. This project I am going to speak to you about started about three and one-half years ago."

"I first spoke with Asia Lynn Fox, before her untimely accident. Recently, I spoke recently with now Grace Fox and also Lois Kelly." "Both women gave me the go ahead to speak with Dr. Sean Kelly and Mr. Bob Williamson."

She softens her speech a little when she asked, "are any of you surprised?"

"This is what I want to announce and provide for the community of Seabeck. My late husband worked for thirty-eight years for the Texaco Company. He purchased stock and bonds, and

bank note after bank note of Texaco Stock."
"Please listen very carefully. I am donating a total
of four-million dollars to Seabeck for the
following uses. One-half million is going to the
Seabeck Conference Grounds for necessary
updates." "This will include additional support for
our beautiful bridge."

"I have gotten approval from the Conference
Grounds for a building to be built on the
Conference Grounds land for a Seabeck Medical
Center and also a Wellness Center providing care,
study and understanding." There is two and one-
half million for the building project and one-half
million for the first year of salaries and necessary
needs."

"Bob Williamson and Sean Kelly came to
Graces and Silas' wedding but they are here too
for other reasons. Dr. Sean Kelly will be in charge
of the Seabeck Medical Clinic and Public Health.
Mr. Bob Williamson, the former President of
Providers of International Care and Education
Foundation will lead the Preventive Care and
Wellness Center."

"Doctor Kelly, in addition of being a gifted
surgeon; also has two Master Degrees, one of them
in Public Health. He is the right man for the job.
Mr. Williamson, after leading a very successful
international health organization for nearly forty-
years is a great asset to have here as well."

"I will ask each of them to come forward to present a short speech." The crowd rose and gave Mrs. Orchards a standing ovation that lasted several minutes. She was all smiles.

Doctor Kelly was the first to speak. "I was more surprised than you are tonight when I first got the call. I talked to my wife and we couldn't turn it down. I have signed a three-year contract." "Keeping this news away from Silas and others has been joyful; there are several former Providers employees we will speak with."

When Bob Williamson spoke, he said that he hadn't decided to take the job until after he saw Seabeck. "Once, my wife and I were here it was a no doubter." "I am anxious to get started and that begins on Monday with interviews with many of you here today." Thank you he said.

I rose from my chair and walked to the microphone and spoke. Amen. There were nearly ten people in Seabeck who knew this was coming down and no one let the cat out of the bag.

I said at the time that Graces' request for an all-community wedding and reception; I thought was a little strange. But this is fantastic news.

Don't you think it is time for Grace and I and others to leave the stage and enjoy dinner. Thank you, my brothers and sisters of Seabeck. Our God is an awesome God. I turned off the mic. I pointed my finger at Grace and she pointed back at me.

To our surprise, waiting to greet us were Della and Jason O'Dea. Introductions were made and after the hugs, Della spoke, "we came now for the wedding but we both wanted you to know that we are coming to Seabeck and we will both be working for Bob Williamson again."

It was Grace who said, "That's outstanding." I agreed.

The Kelly's were next with hugs and Sean spoke that several time, he almost opened his mouth but he had to be quiet until Mrs. Orchards made her announcements.

He also said. "I have asked two of my young, favorite Doctors; MD's if they wanted to come to Seabeck. I expect one of them will." "He will be on my team. There are two nurses living here in Seabeck that work at the Harrison Hospital in Bremerton, who will work with us here. And Janet, will be our scheduler and receptionist when we start.

Lois Kelly spoke. "I am here to do my trade and help anyone the best I can to have them succeed. Including you two."

Horatio and Priscilla walked up and he gave us a blessing in his native Osage tongue. He also said. "My business will be known as: Seabeck's Scenic Slide Show and Gallery."

I told the Nightclouds that we are going to have to make sure that Jasper gets off to a great start with his agriculture adventure. "I am ready to do that." Horatio said.

The two yachts from Shelton were sold to dad and Sean. Horatio bought one in Bremerton and Jasper was lucky and found what he was looking for in Silverdale.

There was a dozen of us who left the Conference Grounds and headed to our house for a toast. Jasper did buy the biggest bottle of Bailey's; I have ever seen. The toast was given with a soft-drink in his hand by Jason Peters. His remarks and blessing were tremendous.

About forty-five minutes, Grace and I were finally alone. I asked Grace if it was time for bed? She spoke. "Yes, if you promise you are not going to go asleep."" This is what I planned for she said." I turned the houses light out. It was a magnificent night.

If the circumstances would have been different; we would have acted differently. It was Sunday and I think fifteen of us went to Lonerock for Chapel. Pastor Taylor greeted all of us, including the Peters and Paster Taylor asked the former Air Force Chaplain if he would come forward and give the opening prayer for the service.

Chaplain Peter's remarks were perfect. He commented on my remarks of the evening before with," Yes. Our God is an awesome God." After the offering had been collected and the bag was full; Pastor Taylor thanked the visitors for being so kind. I hope many of you will come back when you are settled in.

On Sunday afternoon it was time to talk yachts. Grace and I have decided that the name of our yacht would be changed to: Faithful Lady. People loved it. Dad and Brenda's yacht was named: Idahoan. Sean and Lois named their yacht: Harbor Heaven.

Also, Horatio and Priscilla named their yacht: Spanish Lady. Jasper and Janet called their yacht: Wyoming Waves. And finally, the Williamson yacht was named: The Tide Rider. All names were very clever.

Della and Jason cruised with us on the soon to be Faithful Lady. All of the yachts left Seabeck within minutes with each other. It was a beautiful parade of achievements.

There were many cruises when all yachts went together. Some were for pleasure. Others were trips to other communities for dinner outings. Some were for fishing competition and others were just to go as a watchdog when someone else's yacht was being tested. No one never wanted to have to walk home from a yacht trip.

I was one of the lucky ones to see the building plans for the medical facility. It was an "L" shape building of equal size with in and out doors for each facility. There would be parking on two sides; located in front of both entrances. They anticipated a five-month build.

Seabeck was given a great gift from the local builders and only half of the building labor costs would be billed. Anderson windows allowed for fifty-percent savings buying one window, the next one free. There were other gifts as well.

Lois Kelly has turned out to be a super-star. Her designed boards of Graces' clothing line went well. Grace was able to get Nordy's to accept thirteen of twenty-designs presented.

One young Doctor came to Seabeck from Colorado Springs. The two nurses will transfer to Seabeck from Bremerton and I believe that Bob Williamson's team is complete too.

Jasper's company started slow but has picked up well. The equipment all is needed and seems to be passing around to accomplish tasks. Horatio has done several portfolio presentations and his photography for brochures is doing well.

My dad's book has taken some time like he said it would because of the research needed. Brenda is going great guns on her and believes she has a publisher already to handle the call.

There will be fourteen pictures and fourteen artist sketches in my book. Lois, has convinced me to put an artist sketch on the front cover too. Beautiful.

All of the peoples housing needs now have been taken care of. Lonerock is growing as is the choir and for your information; Sean Kelly can sing.

If you are ever in Seabeck, go by the General Store, people there know where any or all of us are living. If you do, one of us will get you a boat ride. As for me. I have turned down employment several times. My writing and my beautiful wife are taking up the majority of my life.

The Seabeck group called a special session and it will be held this evening at my house. The refreshments will be simple and easy to prepare and consume. There will be fourteen people there.

We opened the session with a prayer from Grace. Her prayer was asking God's direction forward placing our relationships with God in his hands. Certainly, asking him for direction and guidance.

It was Sean Kelly, next to speak with us, the fourteen who have chosen Seabeck to seek another Church or to accept the invitation from Pastor Taylor to become members of his Chapel's flock. Dr. Kelly, was in favor of moving forward together in that direction.

My dad, Avery Fox, who spoke, "I was a member of a Christian Church in Moscow for years and I agree it is time now to move on. I am not sure if we should do this as a group but decide on the issue as an individual. As for Brenda and myself; we are more than ready to join the Lonerock Chapel."

I was surprised when Jasper stood and went behind his chair and spoke. "Janet and I would love to have a Chapel where we attended and went the baby is here to have a Pastor Baptist the child. We would love that if it was Pastor Taylor."

By the time that Jasper could sit down, Grace was saying, "A baby?" Janet answered, "Yes, a baby."

It took a couple of minutes for the group to settle in. Jason Robert O'Dea began to speak. "Seabeck doesn't have much of a 'black' community; do you think we would be welcomed?"

Horatio, answered his question in a hurry. "Jason, how many Native Americans have you see here in the community? I am a proud Osage Indian. Priscilla and I are ready to join the Chapel. But I believe that each of us have a right to decide for ourselves.

It was Della, who knocked my socks off again. "Do any of you care that I am black?" "Well, then neither do I." "I say, lets join the Chapel."

I was surprised to hear Sean say, "Let's take a vote." Bob asked. "What will the vote tell us?" I said, remember there will be fourteen who votes.

In my opinion, the vote will tell us how many of the fourteen want to be a part of the Chapel. The people who say 'no' still have their rights to do what they think is right to do. Dad and Brenda were the last to stand. When they did, all fourteen were standing.

On the next Sunday all fourteen of us were welcomed to membership. I was still standing when the rest of the people sat down. Pastor Taylor invited me to come forward for he knew of what I was going to talk about.

When I got to the front of the church. I smiled at him and he said very quietly. "Thank you." Pastor Taylor went back and sat in his chair. The floor was mine. This is so important that I have to do an exceptional job. This will be more difficult than addressing the Prime Minister of Spain.

My sisters and brothers in Christ. I have sad news to convey. On the afternoon of my wedding Pastor Taylor told me his story and asked if I would tell you; the members of the church. I said I would.

It was reported yesterday afternoon, from the Swedish Hospital in Seattle that Mrs. Pamela Taylor has been diagnosed with stage three ovarian cancer. The issues and tissues are spreading rapidly. We must pray every day, multiple times per day for our Heavenly Father to do what is best.

Finding peace and comfort for Pamela is our mission. Our God has brought us together in this house of prayer. Today and into the future we in this house must bring prayer to Pamela and members of her family.

When the service was over, when leaving we all hugged Pastor Taylor. Grace spoke, "the Seabeck women in our group are going to have a 'think tank' session this afternoon on how we can assist the Taylor family, Pastor Taylor directly and most importantly how and what we can do to make Pamela the most comfortable as possible."

I stepped into their meeting in the living room for a couple of minutes and I told the ladies that the guys were going to get her a hospital bed for her home. I quietly went back to the guys outside.

I don't think we should be fishing this afternoon but make the women a delightful dinner. Bob said, "I will go and put a standing rib in the oven." I will make my favorite French onion soup. Sean added. "I got the salad taken care of."

Jasper remarked. "I will do the desert. I will make a German Chocolate Cake." It was dad who added, I will go to the store grab dinner rolls, ice cream and other things I see like a small relish tray.

The discussion with the guys was made to see if there would be other equipment or items that the rental place would have that Pamela could need. Bob spoke, "let's ask them when we call. Where will this be coming from?" Bremerton, I hope.

We learned their three kids would be staying for at least a while with their grandparents in Silverdale. That is a big help for sure. So, we got the telephone number of the grandparents, got them on the line and asked if they needed anything. Their answer was no.

Sean took a written message to Grace that they had at least two hours before we could have dinner prepared for them. Sean said when he returned, "Grace smiled and said thank you."

I called medical supply in Bremerton and got the low-down on the bed and asked what more do you have that we could get by renting? The answer came back, "sheets, blankets, and a blanket warmer." The cost would be two-seventy-five per week. It was Sean who said, "That is reasonable."

I called back and placed an order. It will take two-days before it comes out. This is, as you have heard before is a community made up of thinkers and doers. I called and talked with Pastor Taylor and made arrangements for where the key to the house will be hidden and where would he like Pamela's bed placed in the house. It is going to be the living room. I told him we will be everything in the living room.

I asked Pastor Taylor about Hospice. When the times comes, we need to schedule them for every day at least twelve-hours a day. He spoke, "yes, I want to have an ambulance bring her home when the time comes. I will know more tomorrow."

We all barged into the women's session and gave them an up-date. They did the same for us. The girls will do around the clock care when the time comes in four hours shifts. The girls planned that the husband of the girl on duty would also be in the house ready for anything. We agreed.

It was an hour later when we were ready for dinner. The women took a break and we were asked to join them for the session following dinner and dessert.

Pastor Taylor called me about noon the next day and spoke. "Her outlook is not good but she can come home day-after-tomorrow about noon. Hospice should be notified." They were.

The schedule was set, it will be Grace and me, beginning at noon; followed by Sean and Lois. Others were scheduled too. We added the item of Pastor Taylor dining with us. Pamela would only have liquids.

The ambulance service drove around from Seattle and didn't have to worry about a ferry ride, etc. Pamela was frail and had gone through hell, but appreciated her hospital bed. There were comfortable chairs on both sides of the bed. Grace held one-hand, and the Pastor the other. I sat in the corner.

I suggest reading versus from the Bible and Grace did. Pamala fell asleep almost instantly. She slept a good portion of our shift. When our shift was over; Sean appeared in his hospital grubs. Lois was in casual clothes.

Pastor Taylor, passed a message that her days were very numbered and the children should be brought home for a short time to see their mother still alive. They were coming at noon the following day.

Sean, was seeing things in Pamala that us normal ones didn't see. He stayed into the next shift and Sean and the Hospice lady spoke that the time has nearly come. Pastor Taylor was told and the kids were brought into the room and said their goodbyes. Grace took the little one and walked him into the kitchen for a glass of water. Pamala Taylor, from Seabeck, Washington was with her God within an hour.

All but Sean was excused and he was free thirty minutes later. All others necessary were scheduled within a two-hour period. The people of Lonerock and Seabeck has lost a pillar of strength in the communities. The communities are in mourning.

With that news, I will tell you that the tide is in and you know where I am going. I am going to have my own talk with God and enjoy the sea-air and the beautiful waters of Seabeck. Seabeck is near perfect.

.

EPILOGUE: *FINISHING THE STORY*

Some people want to know if there is going to be a sequel? I don't think so.

I really think that Silas and Grace must have their time together. Avery and Brenda are beginning a union with a past, but they are betting on the future and some fantastic times together.

Dr. Kelly and his wife Lois are going to do Seabeck a world of good. I was on the dock the other day and was looking over Lois' shoulder of the painting she was doing of the Cascade Mountains. Simply, great work from a gifted artist.

Perhaps to the surprise of many is Katarina is spending a lot of time with Pastor Taylor's children. I don't know where that relationship is going.

Asia Lynn and her first husband are gone. Their deaths hurt deeply. Della and Jason have spent a lot of time together and have proven to be professional pair as well as emotionally connected.

Savannah and Alan and their kids will never leave the great Republic of Texas. I acknowledge what the reader wants to know facts about the fiction written. But I want to give them some peace and privacy.

Author Note: It is fun writing when you like and love the people you are writing about. It is like I am living with them.

I will tell you again, Seabeck is near perfect.

ABOUT THE AUTHOR

David Lasswell, has been writing and publishing books since 2006. This is his eleventh book; third novel. He actually lived in Seabeck, Washington up until the fifth grade when the family moved to Port Orchard. The readers love Lasswell's work because he is such a fabulous story teller. The characters created are pure, special, and as real a fictious book can take a persona and personality. Readers of his work, find it hard to believe the characters are not real people. You may compare some of Lasswell's characters to people you think you know.

CPSIA information can be obtained
at www.ICGtesting.com
Printed in the USA
BVHW041248200822
645045BV00001B/49